WELCOME TO THE  HOTEL YALTA

It's bling for your soul!

Daring escapes, backyard firing squads, bowlfuls of goulash, gargoyles, gray skies and bone-chilling cold. From the author of *The Bone Church* and *Welcome to the Hotel Yalta* come these confessions of a Cold War princess.

Get your FREE copy here:
http://victoriadoughertybooks.com/get-your-free-book/

WELCOME TO THE ★ HOTEL YALTA

SIX STORIES OF COLD WAR NOIR

VICTORIA DOUGHERTY

WELCOME TO THE HOTEL YALTA

Published by Wilderness Press

ISBN (paperback)   978-0-9974657-2-3
(ebook)   978-0-9974657-3-0

Visit the author at www.victoriadoughertybooks.com

For those who love the cold.

"Death is the solution to all problems. No man—no problem."

—Joesph Stalin

1956

THE HOTEL YALTA

The ticketing agent's heels squeaked across the linoleum, adding a tinny accompaniment to the man's poor whistling. His shaggy walrus mustache didn't help matters.

"Lístky, tickets, Fahrkarte!" the man droned—a welcome interruption to his little symphony.

Pasha Tarkhan slipped out of his first class compartment, intercepting the weary-eyed fellow.

"*Lístky*," Pasha said, producing two stiff cards from his breast pocket.

The agent appeared a bit ruffled at first, as Pasha loomed over him—more than a head taller, dark and imposing, not the kind of man you'd want to meet alone. But the agent took the tickets, stamping and returning them to the Russian's hand. Avoiding eye contact, he whistled a scarcely recognizable refrain to "Virgin and Whore," an old Czech folk tune, then continued his stroll down the aisle. Pasha took up the song as well, concluding the last, weeping note as the ticketing agent disappeared into the next car.

Pasha looked down at the tickets.

They were neatly stamped with a round ČSSR insignia and a delicate grey cigarette paper was implanted between them. Pasha ran his thumb along its seam. Peering out the aisle window, he caught a glimpse of an old, mustard-yellow farmhouse before it all went dark. The train had entered a tunnel, and the Russian closed his eyes, relishing the grinding rhythms beneath his feet.

Pasha Tarkhan had loved trains since he took his first one from Tbilisi to Moscow when he was sixteen years old. It was a three-day trip that took him through Stalingrad, Tambov, and Tula in the coveted window seat of a crowded compartment smelling of days-old perspiration and live roosters. As a boy who'd never been out of Josefov (population 222), he found every hour of his journey a delight— even sleeping with his cheek sucked against the window like a piece of calf's liver. His sore neck and back was a small price to pay for the opportunity to go to school in Moscow and fulfill his socialist destiny.

He took airplanes and luxury automobiles to most places now, but whenever he had the chance, he booked a seat on the rail. His car and driver couldn't provide him with the shuffling and hard-stepping of the locomotive wheels, the smells of spilled cognac and fine cigarettes that always permeated the first class cabins, and best of all, the unspoiled views of the countryside that even the back roads couldn't offer.

Traveling through Czechoslovakia was a particular treat. The southern part of the country reminded him of his native Georgia, which he hadn't seen in the almost twenty years since he'd left for Moscow. Not the people or the style of housing as much as the rolling hills speckled with wildflowers, and curling rows of trees meandering in and out of the valleys like rivers. The climate was similar, too. The sun felt hotter in the southern Bohemian countryside than it did in Austria, only a few kilometers behind him. Hotter and brighter, like a Georgian summer. He remembered how dark his mother would get when she worked outside in the fields, tending to the sprouting grains.

Poor Mama, he thought. She'd begged him to come

home once more before she died, but he was living in Rome at the time and couldn't get permission to return. To be honest, he hadn't tried. His life had taken him so far away from his farm-boy roots that he had no idea how to come home and explain to his parents and siblings what he'd become. He could've pretended, the way he did every day at work and at embassy functions with his comrades, but his family would've seen through him. His mother, especially, would have known that he was changed and that realization would've put his life in danger. She would've rather seen her son in a gulag in Siberia than have hidden a Judas from Stalin's ever-watchful eyes. Josef Stalin had been her hero, and socialism her religion. In the end, it had been better to let her die with the knowledge that her boy, Pasha, was a high-ranking and trusted member of her government, and that she and her family in Josefov would always get their flour, sugar, and butter for free.

Pasha opened his eyes as the train exited the tunnel and the countryside he'd been delighting in came into view once more. He turned his attention back to his tickets. Reaching into his trouser pocket, he retrieved a packet of fine tobacco—floral and earthen in its scent. He unfolded the little paper between his fingertips and sprinkled the tobacco onto it. As he began the delicate process of rolling his cigarette, he read the neat, black script printed on the grey paper's edge: BICK 3:00 PM TOMORROW.

Pasha ran his tongue over the black ink and finished rolling his smoke. He lit it, taking a deep drag and smiling at his memory of the comely Miss Bick and the safe house she would be offering him the next afternoon. She had tendered her bed in the past as well, but he wouldn't be taking her up on that particular pleasure this visit. The information he would be passing was far too critical for him to don the casual air of an affair, and Pasha didn't want to risk making her feel too at ease with the service she was providing. He would never want a helper to be jumpy and chance attracting attention, but then again, a woman in love could get sloppy and Miss Bick had murmured that endearment into Pasha's ear during their previous liaison. It was a fine line to walk and one he didn't particularly revel in, despite Miss Bick's generosity in tending to his more immediate needs.

Miss Bick. He didn't even know her first name, but she was the kind of woman who would've made a fine wife to a more conventional man. A doctor perhaps. Or a shop-keeper. If only she hadn't decided to involve herself in matters of espionage.

Pasha often wondered if he'd be a happier man if he'd taken a job on the farm where his father repaired tractors. If he'd gone to trade school and chosen the life of a mechanic—a problem solver—his dreams would've remained as simple as his youthful perceptions of Soviet life. He would've married a local girl, had local children, and loved nothing better than the smell of manure baking in the summer sun. The farthest he would travel would be to the Black Sea, where he could rent a cottage for a few rubles and put his feet up. That, instead of going from city to city, meeting to meeting, party to party; drinking vodka and wine and eating rich food to excess while everyone talked of politics.

On one long trip, he'd gotten chest pains and had to be rushed from the Russian Consulate to a large hospital in Rome named after a saint—Saint James, perhaps, but he couldn't recall. The chest pains turned out to be indigestion, but the whole episode hadn't been for nothing. His nurse, Aprilia, had made a marvelous mistress until she married. He made a mental note to himself to send her a cashmere blanket when he returned to Vienna. Her son was almost a month old and all he'd sent so far were flowers.

She'd been the best mistress he'd ever had, from her glorious olive skin to her passionate anti-capitalism, which she loved to extol in front of his colleagues. For a man in Pasha's position, it was important to have a mistress who was either a Soviet sympathizer or simply too stupid to have any of her own opinions.

"Yoo-hoo."

Brandy France peeked her head into the aisle, summoning Pasha back to their compartment. Once there, she guided him down onto the bench and sat next to him, smoothing a crease in her yellow Chanel suit. She wore a matching hat with veil.

"Oh, Pasha, are those poppies? I love fields of poppies."

To Pasha, Brandy looked like a canary bird, but a very pretty one. Thousands of the tiny, red flowers she was admiring were reflected in her eyes, swarming over the grassland, looking all the more vivid against the backdrop of her blue irises. They were a deeper red than even Brandy's painted lips.

"You've seen poppies before—they grow anywhere."

"But they're better here, aren't they? Poppies of the workers' paradise," she chirped, putting her head against Pasha's massive, rounded shoulder.

"Yes, the workers' paradise," he repeated.

Pasha had met Brandy in Rome, where her husband was producing a romantic comedy starring a well-known American actor and an unknown Italian hopeful. For months she offered her crude espionage services to him— talking up politicians at political fundraisers, coming to Pasha with mostly useless bits of jargon that at first he let her blabber to any of his colleagues who would listen. It made him look good that he was able to enlist the enemy, regardless of the caliber of information.

Only weeks after he was transferred to Vienna, Brandy and her husband, Buster, moved there for yet another film. At the time, he thought it was a coincidence.

He was already growing tired of her and planning a graceful exit when she mentioned quite accidentally that her husband had taken to carrying a funny little metal card with the letter "t" engraved on it—"a good luck" symbol, he called it—a prop left over from one of his films. Brandy had followed him to a tiny church near Schweden-platz, where he'd visited a number of times, speaking in hushed tones with a Jesuit there and even donating money. A lot of it. She feared her Jewish husband wanted to convert, but Pasha knew better. In the lining of his suitcase, he carried a similar card, only his was engraved with the Russian word for soul. Its meaning, however, was the same: subversive, spiritualist, and in Pasha's case, traitor, of course.

From that moment on, Pasha couldn't let Brandy go as he'd planned. Furthermore, he had to figure out a way to keep her mouth shut and her visibility low until he could extract himself from the relationship without injuring her pride. For that, he appealed to her overly developed sense of drama.

"The Austrian Premier's wife may have been using the word 'stockings,' but my dear, 'stockings' is the word Western spies commonly use to mean weapons."

"Pasha!" Brandy gasped. "I've heard so many of the ministers' wives use the word 'stockings' in the ladies' room."

Before long, she forgot all about her husband's "conversion" and spent more and more time going to parties at the homes of government officials. It was to Pasha's great relief when Buster France went back to Los Angeles, taking his wife with him. Brandy visited as often as she could, but for the most part she was out of his hair. He even missed her now and then, and her company on the Czechoslovakian leg of his trip would be just enough time spent with her.

"Is it anything like Russia here?" Brandy leaned her head back against the cushion and sighed, humming one, long note. "Russia. Even the word is beautiful. When will you take me there?"

Pasha smiled and moved a platinum blonde curl away from Brandy's eye with his finger. "I think Prague will be better attuned to your interests."

"Oh, my interests are political!" she insisted. "World events. Buster thinks it's an obsession, really, but I'm worried that the whole planet's coming apart. It's all gotten quite out of hand, don't you agree?"

Pasha nodded.

"I've been a lucky woman all of my life. I know I have, and I intend to pass on some of that luck to the less fortunate. We can all make a difference, Pasha. Here I am. Here you are. We're making a difference just by talking about it. Not that I'm all talk. I'm action, too. But action begins with talk and talk begins with thought, thought begins with . . . well, I'm not sure what thought begins with, but it's important."

Brandy lifted her hand to her lips and laughed at herself. She had a throaty, sophisticated laugh—practiced and summoned effortlessly.

"In that case, I'll have to take you to Moscow as soon as possible. Perhaps when my ex-wife takes our daughters to Leningrad."

Brandy hooked her arm through the crook of his elbow and held his hand, intertwining her fingers with his. Her husband, Buster, never listened to her the way Pasha did.

"How much longer until we get to Praha?" Brandy stretched her arms above her head and pointed her toes, yawning. She hated trains.

"Darling, I told you—at least four more hours, and that's without delays. We can be grateful we have no more borders to cross."

"It took so long at the border. Why did it take so long?" Brandy stood up and cracked the window, looking out onto a row of tiny steeples in the distance. The country air didn't cool the compartment enough or ease her claustrophobia. Unbuttoning her jacket, she fanned her breasts with her lapels, finally getting some relief.

"The Soviet Union takes security very seriously." Pasha Tarkhan's last word dropped off as he watched Brandy's champagne silk camisole ripple like water against her skin as she fanned. It was when she moved like this—unconscious and graceful—that he remembered why she'd attracted him.

Pasha tiptoed his fingers over her collarbone, running them down the middle of her torso and onto her leg until reaching her knee. He slid his hand under the fabric of her skirt and up her slender thigh, kissing down the curve of her ear.

"Pasha, what if one of those men come in? They just barge in whenever they want to—I've seen them."

He suckled her entire ear, slipping his fingers into her panties. "They know who I am and have no reason to bother us."

Brandy arched her back and 'mmm'd' like she did after taking her first spoonful of a chocolate mousse—her favorite dessert. "Are you sure?"

Pasha helped her pull off her camisole and bent his enormous head down towards her breasts, kissing each one like he would the tops of his young daughters' heads. "Positive."

She sat up and undid the back of her skirt, then shimmied out of it and kicked it onto the seat opposite them, doing the same with her panties. That left her in only her garter belt, stockings, and yellow patent leather pumps—just how Pasha liked it. He kissed her breasts and belly, then lifted her effortlessly, as if she were merely a glass of champagne, and set her shapely derriere on the window ledge. Brandy loved the strength of his arms, his thrilling combination of brute force and gentility. Pasha slid down until his face was between her thighs, then knelt and let her wrap her legs around his neck.

"Tell me more about what life is going to be like after you conquer the world."

"Oh, darling," he said, trailing kisses up her inner thigh. "It'll be beautiful."

"Couldn't we get a better hotel?"

Brandy stood outside the Hotel Yalta and squinted up at the glimmering, concrete monolith. It looked like a vertical ice cube tray and was positioned in stark contrast to the centuries-old buildings that also lined Wenceslas Square.

"My dear, this is the best hotel in Prague."

Pasha led her inside and was greeted by Veliky, the head of hotel security, who took him in a big bear hug. The two of them went back a long way, having both been stationed in Jerusalem for a brief time at the beginnings of their international careers.

They'd kept up with one another throughout the years, and Pasha had a sneaking suspicion that Veliky was no more a fan of Soviet life than he was. It would account for his less than enthusiastic approach to his work and his move from foreign intelligence to petty hotel spying, which seldom yielded more than an affair between a visiting dignitary and a local shop girl. To his credit, Veliky seemed unembarrassed by his demotion and was in fact thrilled to be back home with a good salary.

"Pasha Tarkhan, it's been over two years. The last time I heard from you, I was in Oslo."

"Bad place for a warm-blooded Moravian."

"A nightmare. As cold as this Goddamn hotel." Veliky whispered. "And who might this beautiful creature be?"

"This is my dear friend Brandy France, who's visiting from America."

"With most loveliest yellow hair I have seen," Veliky gushed, proud of his English. He took her lacquered nails and put them to his lips, kissing each of her fingertips. "Do you have reservation? Think nothing of it if you don't—I'll get you best suite in the house."

Brandy smiled and took a deep, long breath, putting her cheek to her shoulder like a flirt. Pasha was pleased to see her happy at last. From the kitchen, Veliky rounded up the front desk manager, who filled out their reservation card while boasting about the hotel through mouthfuls of smoked mackerel.

"Bulo will take you up to your suite," the manager said, spraying a tiny, half-chewed morsel onto Brandy's sleeve.

Bulo, a young bellboy of about sixteen, neither greeted them nor offered to take their bags until Pasha made him get a luggage cart. Miffed at having to exert himself, he sucked in his pimply cheeks and pouted all the way to their room.

"I'm glad you didn't tip him," Brandy sniffed as the boy

stomped away, but Pasha wasn't listening. He opened the large, metal door of their suite and held it for Brandy as she peeked inside.

The room was as big as a regular suite—in fact bigger, like everything else in the Hotel Yalta—but with hardly any furniture and none of the usual amenities. No bar, no welcome basket or pretty chocolates, and no robes or slippers to get cozy in. Ironically, what little furniture the place had was downright miniature compared to the antique bedroom set in Brandy's Vienna suite. If it weren't for the uniformed bellboys in the lobby—dressed like performing monkeys—the place could have doubled for a sanitarium.

"Don't just stand there, my dear," Pasha said, as he pulled their luggage cart in from the entryway. "Come in."

The suite was a patchwork of beige and white, except for the institutional yellow linoleum in the bathroom. Their two low, single beds had been pushed together and were even harder than the ones in Austria. Brandy sat down and bounced a little on the corner of one of the mattresses. They were as stiff as dry sea sponges. The covers had been pulled tight, like they were in a military barracks, and the pillows were no bigger or softer than the decorative ones adorning the sofas of countless American living rooms. Those might read King and Queen, respectively, and be stuffed with wool. These were plain white and looked to be stuffed with crumpled tissue paper.

"I don't even think I'll be able to fit all of my things into these little drawers," Brandy lamented of the bureau. "That man at the desk bragged that this hotel is state of the art. Better than anything in America. He said it's only been open for a month and pointed to that big banner that read, 'WELCOME TO THE HOTEL YALTA' as if it was some sort of proof. Clearly," Brandy huffed. "The man is a liar."

"And what is it exactly you want me to do? Shall I ask for another suite?" Pasha opened his suitcase and began placing his folded clothes into the top drawer of their bureau, leaving the three drawers beneath it for her. Years of travel had taught him to make himself at home immediately and not live out of his baggage.

"I don't know. Some of the older hotels we passed looked nice." Brandy squinted out of their white nylon curtains onto Wenceslas Square several stories below. "I rather like the look of the Hotel Europa. It seems comfy and pretty."

"The Hotel Europa is falling apart. At least we'll get working faucets here." Pasha eased up behind Brandy and massaged her delicate shoulders.

He wanted to say 'welcome to the workers' paradise,' but he knew the irony would be lost on her. "Hotel Yalta, my dear, is where men of my position stay. It's a monument to socialist productivity and skill." Pasha opened his palms in a grand, presentational style. "How would it look if I stayed in one of the older, bourgeois-built hotels?"

Brandy hung her dresses—a robin's egg Oleg Cassini, a jade Givenchy, and a watermelon Dior—in a wardrobe not much wider than their bureau. "I just don't see why anyone would care who built a hotel and when they built it. And it's not as if this place is cheap. It's just . . . big."

Pasha had forgotten how much Brandy liked to complain. Normally their liaisons supported only a few minutes of talk—thirty at most—as they were short on time and wanted to get down to business.

"Will you excuse me, darling? I'll need to shave before the party tonight. Zablov should be here any minute. You

remember Kosmo Zablov, don't you? He was in Paris before getting assigned here, and used to come to Rome."

Pasha took his razor and shaving soap out of his toilette
case and entered the bath, closing the door behind him.
Brandy heard the faucet turn on and the unmistakable
click of the door lock.

"Pasha . . . " she started, and then thought better of it.
A practiced wife and mistress, she knew a man needed his
privacy sometimes. Brandy didn't really feel like company
right then anyway. She had a splitting headache and was
upset that her clothes were all squashed together in an ugly
wardrobe.

Brandy marched over to her luggage and searched her
Louis Vuitton chest until she found the matching make-
up case at the bottom, under her brassieres. She opened
it, rummaging through her hair combs, toothpaste, mas-
cara, eye shadow, Rouge Classique nail polish, Chanel #5,
Crème la Perle hand cream, night oil, eye balm, sedatives,
her toothbrush, breath mints, countless tubes of lipstick,
and a small vial of 'pick me ups'. She laid every item on the
bed like they were evidence, but among all of her beauty
supplies, powders, and pills there was not one single aspirin
to help relieve the rhythmic pounding at her temples.

"Pasha!" she called out, but he couldn't hear her with the
water running. "Pasha, do you have any aspirin?"

Brandy sat down and put his toilette case into her lap.
She unzipped it and pulled out several medicine bottles,
leaving his hair balm, a comb, and pillbox inside. Amidst
the antacids, laxatives, and boric acid lay a small, brown
bottle of Myer aspirin.

"Pasha, I'm going to have one of your aspirin, okay?
My head's about to split." She opened the bottle and
tipped it over into her hand, but nothing came out. She

shook it, hearing a ping inside, and stuck her pinky into the bottle. "Pasha, I think I'm taking your last one? Is that all right?"

Her pinky dug further until her nail hooked onto something that was sliding against the wall of the bottle. Slowly, she pulled her finger out, dragging with it a long, curly stretch of what looked like camera film, only smaller. She held the film up to the light and looked closely at some tiny, Cyrillic letters printed on what looked to be an architect's drawing. She'd seen one of those when she and her husband, Buster, built their beach house.

"S-P-U-T-N-I-K," she sounded out. Pasha had taught her his alphabet.

"What are you doing?"

Brandy hadn't heard Pasha open the bathroom door and jumped up, dropping the film and the bottle onto the bed with all of her other beauty products. He was standing before her in his royal blue bathrobe with only his trousers on underneath. He didn't look angry exactly, but all of his usual warmth was gone, replaced by nothing but a stare.

"I just wanted an aspirin, that's all. Didn't you hear me asking you?"

"No."

"I'm sorry." Brandy swallowed and looked down at the coiled roll of film. "Do you have any?"

"What?"

"Aspirin?"

Pasha took a deep breath, relaxing his shoulders and letting his features soften. He knew that unless he was smiling, he could look terribly mean. "Of course," he said. "They're in my suit jacket."

Pasha went back into the bathroom and came out a moment later with his suit jacket draped over his forearm.

He handed her a plain, clear bottle of pills and a cup of water, and watched as she took two pills out and swallowed them.

"Thank you," she said.

He nodded.

When she finished drinking her water, he took the cup out of her hands and placed it on the bed table. He walked to the other side of the room and hung his suit jacket on his valet, turned back to her, and grabbed her wrist, abruptly twisting it behind her. He slit her throat with his shaving blade, splattering their white curtains and a bad painting of a grain-processing factory with an arched spray of her blood.

She would die in less than a minute and he was glad. Pasha hadn't wanted her to suffer and made sure that the cut was deep and completely severed her artery. Though she would be unconscious, at least, if not dead, by the time she fell to the beige carpet, he guided her body down slowly and into a position that would be comfortable for her. When she seemed at rest, he went back into the bathroom and washed her blood off of his hands and wrists. The arms of his bathrobe were finished, so he peeled it off, rolled it into a ball, and threw it into the bathtub. He rinsed his arms one more time before putting his white undershirt back on.

Pasha cursed himself for having put the microfilm in an aspirin bottle. He should've put it into his stomach medication, but the Myer aspirin bottle was the same brown color of the film and a safer bet. It had been since before his mistress, Aprilia, that he'd traveled with a woman and he'd forgotten the way they got into everything.

It didn't appear as if she'd gotten a look at the film and she wouldn't understand how to read a blueprint if she had—especially one of a spaceship. But the fact that Brandy had seen it at all sealed her fate. He could've made up a story that she would've believed the way she believed everything else he told her, but that would've been one more lie on top of the many he'd already woven, and he had to draw a line somewhere.

And she was eminently capable of making a slip in front of one of his colleagues or pestering him for a deeper involvement in his so-called patriotic missions for Mother Russia. When the time came to break things off with her completely, she might've even put some of the puzzle pieces together and blackmailed him. It never ceased to amaze him how a woman of limited intellect could become uncharacteristically sharp when her ego had been bruised and her heart broken by a lover. His mistresses had always been fair-minded, but he'd seen it happen before. A more rational man might have killed Brandy after she'd mentioned knowledge of the metal card, but Pasha was an emotional creature, whose heart was made up of poetry. He had a soft spot for his mistresses.

Pasha rolled up the microfilm and put it back in the aspirin bottle, tucking it into his pants pocket. He would be delivering it to the safe house later that afternoon. Plucking Brandy's beauty products off the bed, he placed them in her make-up case according to size, returning it and her clothes to her luggage. Pasha then removed some bogus classified documents—Russian—from the lining of his suitcase and laid them out on the bed in order, throwing a mini-camera—the type used in American espionage—on top of them as if it had been dropped there. He dug a small pistol out of the same lining where he'd stored the bogus documents, and opened Brandy's hand, placing the pistol in her palm and squeezing her fingers around the handle. He always carried props with him in case of an emergency.

Remembering the bathroom, he went to the tub and removed his bloody robe from its cradle, and filled it a quarter of the way with cold water. He was finishing hanging his suit jacket and dress shirt on a rack in the bath when Kosmo Zablov came knocking—late as usual.

"Why aren't you dressed, you ox?" Kosmo feigned outrage when he saw Pasha in his undershirt. He, on the other hand, was dressed in his usual close-fitting, second-rate clothes trying to affect the look of a Venetian gangster.

"What the . . . ?" It was hard to miss Brandy's body and the copious amounts of blood she'd spilled. Kosmo glimpsed her nearly severed head from the doorway and entered the suite to get a better look at her.

"You could've at least saved the artwork, my friend. What did it do to you?"

"She's an American spy."

Kosmo looked down at the surprised look on Brandy's face, and at the gun in her hand.

"This little idiot?"

"No idiot, I'm afraid." Pasha picked the documents up off the bed and held up the camera. "I've been trying to trap her for months."

Kosmo whistled his approval of his comrade's casual air. He assumed the same kind of cool as he eyeballed the contents of the documents in Pasha's hand. "You just leave those around for anyone to find?"

"These?" Pasha held up the documents. He'd enjoyed taunting the agent with them, but it was time to wrap up this whole ugly scene. "These are useless. Go ahead—look at them. I made them up."

Kosmo grabbed them, devouring the first page. "This

is great stuff," he chuckled. "How did you come up with it?"

Pasha shrugged. "I wanted to arrest her, not kill her, but she tried to shoot me."

Pasha went into the bathroom and returned with his suit jacket and shirt. He dressed slowly as Kosmo sat on the edge of the bed and continued to amuse himself with the false documents. He had one foot on the bloodied carpet and one resting on Brandy's shoulder. When Pasha finished tying his tie, he tore the top blanket off the bed and covered Brandy's body with it, making Kosmo put his feet up elsewhere.

"What on earth is this?" Kosmo bent down next to the bed and swept a small, metal rectangle up off the floor. "Soul," he said, reading the tiny script.

Pasha bit down on his lip. He could still detect a faint residue of Brandy's sex in the corners of his mouth. "It's mine," Pasha told him. It must have fallen out of his suitcase lining when he removed the fake documents. "She gave it to me as a symbol of—oh, I don't know—love, I guess. You can have it if you want."

Kosmo chuckled, tossing it on the bed. "Love," he repeated.

Pasha went to the vanity and applied a light dab of Chanel Pour Monsieur to his neck—a gift from Brandy. He stepped back, appraising himself as casually as he could.

"Have this cleaned up, will you?" he said. "I need to go downstairs and request another suite—one with a clean carpet."

"You are a cold bastard, aren't you?" Kosmo stood up, slapping Pasha's back before going over to the telephone. "I'll get right on it. You know this is going to get some attention. She's a Hollywood type—the denials will be fervent and angry."

"We have the evidence right here—they can deny it all they want."

Kosmo Zablov smiled, revealing his crossed front teeth. "What the hell?" he said, picking up the receiver, "I've always loved to annoy the Americans."

He dialed the three-digit number, but the front desk was busy.

"Of course, you'll be sent back to Moscow for this," Zablov continued. He dialed again and this time the line rang. "And you'll miss your dinner with the French president next week. Bastard—you always get the greatest of the great boondoggles. President Coty has the most exquisite chef—or so I've been told."

Pasha Tarkhan nodded and tried his best at a smile. "I always end up back in Moscow sooner or later."

"Don't we all?" Kosmo Zablov lamented, placing his fingers over the mouthpiece.

The phone stopped ringing and a bored voice came on the line. "Yes, hello, front desk?" Zablov inquired. "We have a dead mouse up here."

A LEGACY OR A
RESIDUE

The rosy sun skimmed the water, as if dipping its toe to test the temperature. The simple beauty of the sky made Lily smile. It was one of the few uncomplicated things in her life right then. The sun, the water, and Etor, the hotel gigolo, who sat beside her imparting his particular brand of wisdom.

"A woman should never travel alone," Etor chided. "Especially one of childbearing age."

Lily chuckled at how he could sound like a prim schoolmaster, all the while sporting a most fashionable pair of chartreuse swimming trunks that left little to the imagination. She tossed her head back, enjoying the tickle of a lone droplet of sweat that rushed down from her neck and into her cleavage.

"I'm not alone," she teased. "I have you."

Etor had taken to joining Lily around sunset, sitting cross-legged on the rocks, as they watched jellyfish bob on the swelling surface of the Pélagos Sea. His lined face was still handsome, but Lily figured he was only a couple of years shy of retirement, as men half his age courted the attention of the same vacationing countesses who used to buy Etor's supper and handmade Italian shoes. The ladies were only a decade or so older than the bronzed Cretan now, and stared with growing resentment at the silvery roots of his auburn hair.

"You need a man," Etor asserted. "A Greek man. The Americans can't handle you."

Lily had had a man. Richard. Of the Philadelphia Putnams, not the Boston Putnams, as he'd been quick to point out.

Aquamarine eyes, a thick, ungovernable mane of honey and rust hair, and a mother who hummed "Tangerine" as she sneered at Lily through her gin and tonics. Pooh was her name, of all things. Pooh, short for Abigail. Pooh, as in *Oh, Pooh. No, Pooh!* And *Pooh, you didn't!* Pooh, who'd talked of Richard's old girlfriends—girls who hadn't seemed quite right to her in their time—with a breathy nostalgia usually reserved for the one that got away. And Pooh, who had bullied her son into law school and dangled that victory in Lily's face like a diamond watch. Never mind that Richard would make a terrible lawyer, at least as Lily saw it. Even if he did continue to breeze through his studies with the same ease that he claimed to absorb Byron.

Poor Richard. He has the soul of an artist, his friends would say. *Although not the talent,* Lily had wanted to add on more than one occasion after their relationship had begun its slow flush down the pink porcelain toilet of his mother's new powder room.

Poor Richard, he's too much of a gentleman to give that Greek girl the heave-ho now that it's come this far. No one actually said it—that Lily knew of—but the sentiment was there. It was the uninvited guest at every party she and Richard attended together, every family dinner; unrelenting in every look, polite question, and feigned interest in what Lily was reading. Even that was subject to censure in the most well-bred possible way, naturally. It was, to the people in Richard's circle, unseemly for a woman to enjoy Bellow, Hemmingway, O'Connor, or Nabokov, God forbid.

But it wasn't Richard's friends who really got to Lily in the end. It was the barely concealed look of relief on Richard's face the night she "released him from their engagement" that Lily found so damned infuriating. His crafty, humiliating way of manipulating her into doing his mother's will.

Spineless bastard.

"Lilia, Lilia, Lilia," Etor yawned, splashing his suntorched chest with palmsful of chilly salt water.

Lily patted Etor's shoulder and ran her fingers through her waist-length hair. The thick, black threads tangled around her knuckles, as day upon day of sunbathing was making her ends brittle.

"Would you mind?" she asked, removing a tall vial of olive oil from her beach-bag. Etor sprinkled the oil over her hair, massaging it into her dry ends.

"Of course Kástro is no place to find a husband," Etor reminded her. "Only adulterers and seducers come here."

Kástro, or Old Town Monemvasia, as it was known to tourists—was notorious for offering what the flashier getaways never could—secrecy. Lily had nothing to hide on this—her *last*, she swore to herself—trip to the tiny peninsula, but she had plenty to hide from. And it wasn't just a broken engagement; one that came with the added embarrassment of having to admit once again that she was a screw-up when it came to matters of the heart. *No*, Lily realized, the heart was too specific a category. Most people back home just thought she was a screw-up. Period.

It was why she'd grown to hate Boston. And the whole Eastern seaboard, except for New York. Because despite how hard she'd tried to fit in—at Dana Hall, at the god-damned Junior League—Lily just couldn't stand the stuck-up, intellectual pomposity of the men, or the prim, icy-cool affectations of girls who moved in cliques so armored you needed barbed wire cutters just to say hello. The same girls who feigned propriety with the right kind of boy from seven to nine p.m., then slipped a cute waiter a little note about where to meet for some real fun. Lily knew all too well that she wasn't the only girl at Dana Hall who'd had more than the prescribed three lovers you could take and still remain vaguely respectable. The snooty pricks who'd wooed her onto their plaid couches knew that, too, but it didn't matter. All that mattered was that she wasn't one of *them*.

She'd thought Richard was different.

And he was, at first. Late night coffees, introducing her to poets she pretended not to know, finding her family funny and eccentric instead of brash. Richard was the only non-Greek guy who'd ever had the guts to take Lily home; she had to give him that. But putting up with the long silences, the droll weekends at his parent's "beach" house—a place set on the frigid, un-swimmable waters of Northeast Harbor, Maine—had proved to be too much. For both of them.

Her father told her not to think much about Richard of the Philadelphia Putnams. He was destined to spend his life in old money oblivion, breathing rarified air and eating bland food.

Not like her, Daddy said. Lily was the daughter of a Hellene. One who came to America at fifteen—alone—and made his own way. Theron Tassos had worked the docks, then the avenues and the markets, among other things, while the fathers of boys like Richard sipped their brandies and talked of the world's stage as if they were on it as anything more than a ceremonial ribbon.

Malakas, her father called them. *Jerk-offs.*

They may have been just that, but it didn't change the fact that Lily's father thought too highly of her. If Lily was the mighty Hellene in Theron Tassos' fantasies, she would've never tried to gain entry into Richard's world in the first place—pining for their stamp of approval like a hungry beagle. She would have never put up with the not-so-subtle inquiries, *Are you going to wear that to Mother's?* The dry, fervent kisses followed by the panted pleas to *go down.* That was something the Betsys and Lindys of Richard's world didn't do. Not well, anyway.

"Go to Greece," her father had urged. "A few weeks on the Peloponnese will remind you of who you are."

Only it hadn't. It didn't. It wouldn't.

Greece, while a virtual banquet of indulgences, had never been a place of clarity and motivation for Lily. Come to think of it, no place had. Not even New York, with its busy inhabitants who reveled in variety—enjoying life like they would an assortment of *frutti di mare* on a big silver plate.

Furthermore, what Lily hadn't counted on was how well Kástro in particular kept its confidences. The rocky cape trapped them like ghosts in a long-abandoned cemetery, and as Lily walked the winding trails and footbridges, nearly every blooming bush and medieval ruin murmured a story of some time or another when Lily had ended up flat on her back with her dress hiked above her hips.

"What place could be more pleasing to the senses?" Etor beamed, uncorking a bottle of Malvasia wine as he beheld his adopted home.

"Please," Lily yielded, and Etor poured a liberal serving into her pewter goblet. She swished it around, watching the wine twirl.

"You don't have time to sit on Monemvasia for weeks like a Danish tourista," Etor insisted. "By age twenty-five you won't be marketable anymore."

Lily looked at her watch and nodded. "I don't know that I was meant for marriage," she said aloud, but not specifically to Etor. Lily had never been in love. And the only man who'd ever really cared for her was her father—a man whose tender bearing at home and zeal for his family felt at times like Lily's only true tether to her heart. Of course, his dealings with the outside world were less benevolent, she'd learned.

"Miss Lilia!" Stavros, the concierge called. "A note for you."

Stavros waved the sealed envelope in his hand as he teetered over the melon-shaped rocks. He nearly tumbled into the water twice, as if he didn't make the journey from the Hotel Malvasia's lobby to the seaside at least a dozen times a day.

"It just appeared on my desk," he marveled. "I didn't see who could've left it."

It was a plain, white envelope—the size of an invitation—and *Miss Lilia Tassos* was scribbled on the back, looking more like *Miso Lihila Tssas* to the untrained eye.

"Thank you, Stavros." She tucked the envelope into her beach bag, and looked back at the jellyfish, which were now floating out to sea.

"Open it," Etor demanded. "It could be from an admirer."

Lily smiled at the Cretan gigolo, retrieving the envelope and then tearing it at the seam. She pulled out a short note scribbled in the same slapdash handwriting. Tucked inside its crease was a simple, metal card with a plus sign embossed on one side and a six-pointed star on the other. It was the size of a calling card and engraved with eight tiny Cyrillic letters.

"Well?" Etor pressed. Lily patted his hand.

"No admirer, I'm afraid. Just a man."

Tony Geiger sat on a partial fortress wall that looked down over the sea and a rocky perch that Lily Tassos had fled around dinner time—a tawdry Greek Romeo on her tail.

Tony had hiked up from the waterfront an hour early to sit amongst the ruins at the top of the peninsula and smoke Chesterfields in the cool evening air. The night required a light jacket, but Tony had under-dressed on purpose. It kept him sharp when he'd had a lousy night's sleep—taking the red-eye from Berlin to Athens and then driving another five hours to Monemvasia.

"*Fuck*," he said, flicking his last good cigarette into a bush of wildflowers. He watched the butt glow like a lightening bug, then fade under the frizzy bloom of the white buds. He wished he could buy a decent pack of smokes in Greece.

"Well, it's about time," he murmured as he watched Lily scramble up a corkscrew rock path from behind a collapsed church wall. She was twenty minutes late and dressed in what looked like a white linen bathrobe that flew behind her like a spinnaker. Though he knew and understood fashion and finery, he'd never learned to appreciate it.

"Tony," she called.

Lily had the kind of looks Tony could appreciate, complete with a big nose and a full set of lips that saved her from cuteness. As far as he was concerned, she wrecked everything she had going for her with flashy clothes and too much perfume. Despite her Boston upbringing, she looked and behaved like a new-money Greek.

"You might as well go ahead and blow my vacation," Lily grumbled, stumbling over the broken castle steps.

Geiger rubbed the thick stubble on his cheeks and shook his head.

"Come on, Lily. What's a girl like you got to take a vacation from—shopping?" He smiled and folded his arms. "Besides, something vaguely resembling a job might actually be good for you. Get you away from the Lotharios that hang around in places like this."

Lily put her palms to her temples then shook her hands as if she were chasing away an odor. She caught herself smiling at him and changed her look to a smirk. "It's amazing what a girl will do for a guy who keeps threatening to put her daddy in jail."

Geiger pushed away from the fortress wall and pointed a finger in her face. The force of the gesture caused Lily to stumble backwards and trip on her white linen train. He grabbed hold of her arm before she could fall and drew her close. "Your father's an arms dealer, lady!"

He let go of her and glanced around them. Geiger then leaned back onto the stone wall, spitting over his shoulder and watching his foaming saliva disappear over the cliff-side into the black air.

"You should thank me for letting you keep living this life of yours. You understand treason? How about seizure?" Geiger hoped the Greek baron would eat a bullet one day and figured that sooner or later, he would. "What's it gonna be, Lily?" he said.

Lily tucked her hair behind her ear. She hated it when Geiger popped up out of the blue like this. The funny little errands he'd sent her on—going to the Russian Tea Room at exactly 5:15 pm wearing a red skirt or leaving her purse at the Seven Sisters tube stop in London—weren't much more than an inconvenience, but his brown eyes told a much longer story than his thirty years, and the way he sucked in his cheeks whenever she started talking made her feel like the kind of woman she feared she was—bored and rich, with the wrong kind of money. Lily had seen enough to know that wasn't the way she wanted to spend her life, but she wasn't sure what options there were for a girl like her.

She looked at Geiger—into his eyes, which she often avoided—and nodded her head. "What have you got for me this time?"

Tony Geiger reached down and moved a fallen stone about the size of a gold brick. He produced another envelope with Lily's name on it; this one long and thick with folded papers. Lily grabbed the envelope and opened the flap, pulling out an airline ticket, itinerary, visa, and various receipts in her name. "This is going to Moscow."

"You're going to Moscow," Geiger corrected.

"Why would I go to Moscow?"

Geiger scratched his head and shrugged his shoulders. "All the good parties are happening in Moscow these days—the rich Pinkos love it."

"I'm not a Pinko."

Geiger smiled, for once looking sweet, lighthearted and his age. "Lily, you're not an anything."

Something inside her wanted to smile back at him despite the insult, but instead she rubbed her lips together as if she were redistributing her lipstick. "Moscow, huh?"

"A little sightseeing—Lenin's Mausoleum and all that.

You know you can view his actual body in Red Square. The Bolshevik Fuehrer."

"That's disgusting."

"No, I've seen it. He doesn't look that different than he does in photos." Geiger lit another smoke and inhaled deeply. "You still got that little present I sent you?"

Lily tucked her index finger into the bust of her dress and slid the odd metal card he'd conveyed through the hotel concierge over her collarbone. The gesture was meant as a joke—a play on something you might see in a French movie—but Tony Geiger didn't even smile.

"Don't lose that," he warned. "It's more important than your passport."

Lily took the card and flipped it over a couple of times, running her index finger over the Cyrillic lettering. She'd thought of taking Russian at Wellesley, hoping to rule the cocktail party circuit with unfiltered phrases from *Anna Karenina,* but ended up learning Arabic instead. Languages were the only thing she'd ever been really good at and she collected them the way some people collected amusing dinner guests.

"It looks like a belt buckle," she remarked.

Geiger shook his head. "For your purposes, it'll get you a suite at the best hotel in Moscow, provided you show it to my good friend Fedot at the front desk. It'll also help you know who your friends are."

Lily mouthed "Fedot" and shrugged her shoulders. "And?"

"And, on a separate note, you're now a member of the American Communist Party. Back-dated three years, of course. Like you joined in college."

This time Lily laughed out loud. "What if the Ruskies find out I'm not?"

"Oh, but you are. I've made sure of it. It makes getting you into Russia all the easier. And getting you out a little more interesting."

Lily stopped laughing and squeezed the card in her palm until one of its pointy edges dug into her skin. She held it up between two fingers and then flicked it at him. Geiger caught it.

"Are you out of your mind?" she said.

"Lily, keep it down."

Lily paced in front of Geiger and then stopped, pointing her finger in his face the way he had to her. The wind was turning wild and cold, blowing her dress every which way. She wished she hadn't worn it. "Is this about my father? Or is it about something else?"

If only, Geiger thought.

"Your father's in Boston and he's not going anywhere that I know of—you can call him if you want. And as for something else?" Tony folded his hands together as if he were praying. "Look . . . it's not even on my radar."

Lily hardly ever thought about that night in New York anymore, either. Until she thought about it, that is—the night she'd first met Tony and assumed, wrongly, that it was by chance. He'd approached her outside of her hotel as the bellman hailed her a cab. He said he was late and asked if he could share the ride.

They talked about the weather—it had been lousy—and about Faulkner—whom they both loved. Then he asked her out for a drink. It occurred to her, as she found herself making love with him standing up behind a beer truck outside of Chumley's, that he'd lied about being late for an appointment. She could never, for the life of her, understand how it was that men knew they could have her without even the polite formality of a hotel room.

Then Tony just stopped in the middle of everything.

"You want to go somewhere else?" he asked.

In the cab back to the St. Regis she found he spoke Greek and Italian in addition to German and Hebrew. She didn't speak Hebrew, but they took turns impressing each other with the languages they had in common. They also shared a love of black comedy and Tony told her that he'd never actually met a woman with a real sense of humor. He said that women he'd known liked laughing at jokes, but rarely made any.

Somehow, though, despite all of the laughing and the teasing and the fact that she was pretty sure she was the best-looking girl Tony had ever gotten into bed, they "couldn't close the deal" as he mumbled right before passing out. He blamed the two bottles of wine they'd shared when they got back to his suite, but he hadn't seemed all that drunk to her.

Now, as she looked at him—a year and some later—he seemed a hell of a lot older than he had then.

She watched as Tony Geiger bent down and picked up the metal card she'd flicked to the ground. He dusted it off and held it flat in his hand as if it were some kind of peace offering, the lines on his palm looking like deep scars.

"Lily, I don't like your father very much, but I've got nothing against you. This is just something you can do pretty easily for me, that's all."

Lily rolled her eyes at him, but instead of Tony giving her some smart-ass comment, he looked down and swallowed hard. "Look," he said, meeting her eyes again. "I need you to do this for me."

Geiger stepped closer to her and held his hands up as if he were going to put them on her shoulders. For a second, she thought he was going to kiss her. And for a second, he wanted to.

"You'll walk around for a couple of days, go to a party or two, and on the third day you're there—three minutes before noon—a man with a doctor's bag is going to ring the bell at your suite. When he arrives, you'll show him the card, go to the safe in your chest of drawers, and give him the contents. The combination will be your birth date. Easy to remember."

"I don't need it to be easy—I remember everything."

"Yeah, you do, don't you?" Tony said. It was funny to him how she remembered every line from every book she'd ever read. It was not funny how he remembered the soft curve of her hips and the way her toes tasted in his mouth. "Anyway, you can go home any time after that. Or stay and see Mr. Lenin's mummy if you want."

Lily backed up and eyed Geiger from close-cropped hair to tightly laced shoe. This was definitely different from the other times, and Lily didn't like it. Tony was edgy and distant—but as if he was acting that way on purpose. It wasn't like he was a soft, warm blanket the other times they'd met, but he wasn't stiff either and could laugh here and there, even if it was at her expense. She wondered if everything else until now had been a warm-up—a series of little tests meant to help him discern whether or not she could cross a line. And she wondered whether Tony ever acted real at all.

God, she was sick of men. "I'm going back to my hotel."

"Lily!" Geiger called, as she turned on her heel and stomped to the slim path leading back to the castle. A thorn flower bush caught the painted silk scarf Lily had tied around her waist and the wind blew it off the tiny dagger of a petal, catching it around Tony Geiger's ankle.

"Lily! Are you going to leave a legacy or a residue?"

Lily stopped and spun around.

Geiger opened his palms and smiled like he meant it.

This," he said, holding up her airline tickets, "is a legacy." Tony Geiger bent down and retrieved her scarf, letting it flail in the air. "What do you think a thing like this is? Bet it cost a pretty penny, but what's it worth?"

Lily rolled her eyes and turned back towards the path. It was one of her favorite scarves—and it had cost a pretty penny—but he could keep it.

"Who'd you tell, Lily?"

Lily stopped and cocked her head.

"What?"

"Who'd you tell I was here?"

"Nobody."

Tony Geiger took a step forward and wobbled a little bit. He closed and opened his eyes like he was shaking off a hang-over, then fell over onto his face.

"Jesus. Tony!"

Lily sprinted over and knelt beside him, running her hand down the length of his back. Something small and shaped like a pen cap was stuck between his shoulder blades. She pulled it out and saw that the thing had a thick needle that protruded from the top. Lily gasped and threw it to the side.

"Can you talk?" she asked him.

Tony's eyes were open and his lips were still moving— not as if he was trying to tell her something, but rather in a struggle to keep breathing. She took his hand on impulse, holding it and squeezing his fingers until Tony Geiger was gone and she was alone.

"I didn't," she whispered. "I didn't tell. I swear."

Lily wanted to cry, but her head wouldn't let her. She

stood up and rubbed her eyes, inching cautiously back from Tony's corpse as she watched the sky and the sea. They mingled together into one black mass that could only be distinguished by sound—a whistle of the wind and whoosh of the waves.

"Oh, God," she murmured.

She looked down into Tony's face and swallowed a sickening pool of saliva that had collected under her tongue. It almost made her vomit. "Dear God," she said fully aloud this time. Tony's eyelids were half-closed, like he was falling asleep to the sound of a radio show. Lily thought about what it was Tony might like to listen to when he was alone. Maybe one of those detective stories her mother was so fond of.

"God-damn," she shouted. She'd drank with Tony and made him laugh. She fed him pieces of smoked trout from room service china. He'd been inside her, for Christ sake!

And he'd been one of the good guys. Maybe Lily didn't know all that much about the dead man at her feet, and maybe she hadn't loved him, but part of her wished she had. Because if there was one thing that she was one hundred percent sure of, it was that in the big picture Tony was okay. More than okay.

"Bastard—where are you?" she gasped. She squatted down, waiting, watching.

Nothing changed—at least not out there. Inside, though, she could feel the shift, the adjustment from her old life—the one with Etor and Malvasia wine and without a thing to do—to her new one.

The new one she knew nothing about, except that a CIA agent was dead on top of the ruins of Monemvasia and she was hunched there on a cliff with a billowing, white dress on—an easy target for another poison pen cap. Lily took in a sharp breath and started untying her belt and fumbling with her buttons. Her fingers were shaking and wouldn't cooperate, so she grabbed the top of her dress at the neck and yanked as hard as she could, until half the buttons popped off and it fell to her ankles. Her tanned skin blended well with the night air and she figured at the very least Tony's killer would have a hard time distinguishing her from a Greek fir. Lily ducked behind the eroded fortress wall and pulled her airline tickets and the metal card from under Tony's fingers.

Running naked back to her hotel room, Lily did not go un-noticed in the Hotel Malvasia's lobby. But this was Kástro, after all, and there was little that could have surprised the hedonistic clientele or jaded hotel clerks.

Once inside her room, she locked the door and drank three shots of ouzo—compliments of the house. Out her window, the one she'd left open for fresh air, Lily saw the same panorama she had admired earlier in the evening after she and Etor had returned from the seaside. The little lane, two floors down, had been bustling, a stream of worshipers filing out of the only church on Monemvasia—a small Greek Orthodox temple with a domed roof shaped like a breast. Now, the lane was gloomy and still, with only the click-clack of a pair of high-heeled sandals sounding off of its cobblestones. The footsteps seemed ominous, like they could have, conceivably, belonged to Tony's killer and Lily shuddered.

After closing the window and locking the latch, Lily crouched down and slithered beneath her bedframe, pulling with her the copper spine of her bedside lamp and the coverlet from her mattress. She balled the soft, cotton spread into her arms like a loved one and hid under her bed in the dark—naked, but with her wits about her—until the sun rose out of the sea and filled her room with its butter and lemon glow. It was there, under her bed, and in a fetal position, that Lily got hold of herself and made some decisions about her life.

STEPPING ON THE THROAT OF HIS OWN SONG

Kosmo Zablov had no grasp of situations in their whole, though he could execute flawlessly against any detail that protected or advanced his own self-interest. He had never questioned his instincts in this regard and certainly never considered any moral implications.

But right at this moment, he would have given anything for the mental agility that could've freed him to apply his gifts of self-preservation to the mechanics of his actual job. It seemed like such a small leap and yet somehow he had never mastered it. If only Kosmo could have been more like his brother.

"Lucky Yakov," the spy bemoaned, as he pulled his overcoat closed and descended into the Prospect Mira metro station.

Yakov was a journalist, and one of some repute, who was always writing stories about exemplary Soviet scientists or engineers. It amazed Kosmo how his older brother never failed to convince himself that he possessed the same dexterity as his subjects and could've easily—if he had fancied—become, say, a prize-winning physicist, instead of someone who simply interviewed physicists.

But this was a moot point.

Zablov's problem was made worse by the fact that he had no insight into his one and only talent, either. It wasn't a skill he had practiced and perfected, the way Yakov had mastered three-act journalistic structure. As a result, he didn't know how he had come to the decisions he had made or why things had always worked out for him.

And unlike his good brother Yakov, Kosmo Zablov had no inclination towards self-delusion. He knew very well that he had risen in the ranks of the KGB by manufacturing espionage escapades that allowed him to save the day, and passing off the blame for the very real exploits he had overlooked. Politics and intrigue were where Zablov's core abilities lay, and it was imperative that he rise out of the KGB and into areas of diplomacy. There, his inadequacies could take years to surface.

For the time being, however, he still had to deliver real results and his terror of getting caught "improvising," as he liked to call it, was starting to wear on him.

The nightmares, the tremble in his pinky finger, the days of insomnia before any meeting with a superior, and the crushing lower back pain that seemed to start at his arches and shoot up to his buttocks before lodging itself at the base of his spine, had all intensified as expectations of him increased and he began to be considered for the very positions he had been striving for, but never seemed to get offered.

Finally, not two weeks before, Comrade General Pushkin had revealed to him that a diplomatic post was indeed in his future, but not for another two to three years. By then, Pasha Tarkhan would be tendered a seat at the big table in Moscow and Zablov could succeed him on the Lobster and Lafite circuit, as it was called.

"Only the '45. The remainder of the 40s Bordeaux are dreadful," he mimicked Tarkhan's Georgian accent to himself.

Two to three years was an eternity under his present circumstances! Not only could an associate stumble upon his shortfalls, but a foreign agent could exploit them as well. He'd seen it happen before.

"I'd rather compose romances for you—more profit in it and more charm. But I subdued myself, setting my heel on the throat of my own song," he whispered the Mayakovsky poem, almost laughing, as a fat-faced hag turned at the sound of his voice. Zablov elbowed his way past her on the stairwell.

Poetry—Mayakovsky's—soothed him; it was the way the words pranced from his tongue and out into the ethos as if he'd composed them. If he was Yakov, he would be certain that he could have, had he not turned his eye towards journalism, of course.

It pleased Zablov to remind himself of his brother's shortcomings. Particularly as he struggled to shake the curly-headed man with the dented face General Pushkin dispatched to follow him. The Neanderthal had made no effort to hide his intentions and strolled around the metro station—hands in his pockets, admiring the Cathedral ceilings and giant Deco chandeliers –until he hopped onto the same coach Zablov had boarded.

"Try this, you box-eyed bastard," Zablov grunted as he muscled his way out of the train car's sliding doors just before they squeezed shut, and jumped onto another train bulleting in the opposite direction. Pushkin's thug was left wedged behind him—stuck on a coach to Oktyabrskaya.

Zablov needed all the time he could steal in order to get in and out of the secret apartment he kept in Leningradsky Prospect. It had been a stroke of genius on his part to secure the place for his own use—genius and blind luck. The one-bedroom flat had been formerly used to spy on a biologist who ended up brain-dead after a drunken skiing accident. Instead of having the flat reassigned, Zablov had burned all files on the ill-fated scientist and transferred the authorization of residency to a man he'd invented.

While the flat was hardly the type of place he would take anyone but an indiscriminating slut, it did possess one critical perk: It had a working telephone.

"Immediately, please. I want to place a call to Heraklion, Greece." Zablov used his best Belarus accent to disguise his voice. All outgoing and incoming calls were recorded and deliberated upon *ad nauseam* by young intelligence officers eager to make a name for themselves. Zablov had spent his first two years out of school scribbling just such painstaking notes and exaggerating the significance of mostly banal conversations.

He hung up the phone and waited for the operator to call back, hoping against hope that for once the Moscow switchboard would operate with a modicum of efficiency. There was no food in the cupboards, only a few satchels of tea, so Zablov prepared a cup and sat a few feet away from the window.

"Mother of God!" he yelped, nearly falling off the old piano stool that served as the only chair in the flat. Pushkin's thug—with his smashed-in face and gait like a rhinoceros—was lumbering down Tverskaya Street, his shape unmistakable under the lamplight. He nodded at an old woman carrying a beehive satchel, and crossed the street, looking up at Zablov's apartment.

"Bastard!" Zablov cried, crouching to the floor. It would've been impossible for the thug to see him, but he was taking no chances. The spy reached up and dialed the phone again, peeking just over the windowsill to glimpse the top of the thug's head as he entered the building.

"International operator," he begged. It took a little under four minutes for a normal man to walk up to the ninth floor. This allowed time for a half minute rest on the sixth floor and the eighteen paces it took from the top of the staircase to Zablov's apartment door.

"Operator, I called a few minutes ago regarding a line to Greece. Yes, yes, I know." Zablov held his palm over the receiver and took two deep breaths before resuming. "This is an extreme emergency, you see. My mother is very ill. It can be any moment now."

He nodded his head as the operator explained procedure and ground his knuckle into a groove on the telephone table. "Yes, I'll hold."

He imagined the thug's breath getting more labored with each stair—taken two at a time at first, but not slowing down.

"Another minute, you say?"

It occurred to him suddenly that he hadn't devised what he was going to tell the Cretan gangster. He couldn't reveal the truth for obvious reasons—the bald menace had already pocketed his fee and couldn't care less about the mess Zablov had stumbled into.

Great news, my friend! You can tell your man I won't be requiring his services—not this time, anyway. Zablov tried it on, but it was wrong. A man like that—with his pair of thick-fingered hands created for one and one only purpose—would never buy it.

Call it off, unless you want to lose your only advocate in Moscow.

"No," Zablov murmured. Far too much information, and no guarantee that he was the Cretan's only advocate.

You're in danger. Call it off.

"Perfect."

The message was simple and mysterious—just the right combination to motivate the paranoid mind of a criminal.

"Yes, I'm still holding," he stuttered. Zablov put the telephone receiver down and crept to the foyer. He held his breath as he put his ear to the door, as if any noise he made could be yet another piece of evidence against him. He could hear, on the seventh floor, the unmistakable thud of a pair of police boots, mounting the stairs at a stoutly pace. The thug was making excellent time, and had clearly foregone the need for a rest. Zablov's shoulders dropped, surrendering into a slouch. The catalog of his alleged crimes, he realized, was impressive: treason, conspiracy, murder. He could even hear himself listing the evidence against him, as Jarko, his enforcer, stood behind him with a truncheon.

Isn't it true you met with Pasha Tarkhan in Prague?

Isn't it true you were his accomplice in treason against the Soviet Union?

Isn't it true that you hired an assassin to have Pasha Tarkhan murdered before he could corroborate any evidence against you?

"Horrific coincidence," Zablov wailed.

It was, to Zablov, profoundly unfair that a mere scheme for a promotion had entangled him in much larger events that he had so little control over. If he'd even suspected that Tarkhan was a double agent, he would've made other plans! He certainly wouldn't have had drinks with the man in Prague at the damned Hotel Paris, where everyone and their third cousin could have spotted them.

"Mother," he cried, his eyes searching the pock-marked plaster of the ceiling. Zablov didn't know why he called for her. She'd always loved Yakov better.

Tender souls! You play your love on a fiddle, and the crude club their love on a drum. But you cannot turn yourselves inside out, like me, and be just bare lips!

He invoked Mayakovsky—though not out loud this time. Just to himself.

Zablov took a sip of his tea and reached into his wallet, taking out a small, twenty-six-year-old newspaper clipping. It showed a picture of Mayakovsky—twenty-two, but looking forty. The article went on to detail his unfortunate end: age thirty-six, playing Russian roulette until he lost.

Both poet laureate and shameless Bolshevik flack, Mayakovsky had always fascinated Kosmo Zablov, and the spy now found disturbing parallels between his own life and that of the young, brooding poet's. Zablov gazed closely into his imagined counterpart's eyes. Even then, when he was in the thrall of his Bolshevik hallucinations, Mayakovsky's eyes looked doomed, and Zablov wondered if his own eyes, at twenty-two, told a similar tale.

The soft rap at the door came in tandem with a voice that was at once kindly and willing to understand. Zablov had heard such a voice a thousand times during various interrogations.

"I'll be right with you," Zablov called. "Let me just get a robe."

Kosmo Zablov gulped the remainder of his tea. It was hot and stung the back of his throat. He flitted to the window, opening it wide and peering all the way down onto the concrete walk spotted with dog feces.

Tucking Mayakovsky's worn portrait into his breast pocket, he eased his buttocks onto the window ledge.

"Comrade Zablov, are you alright?" the voice called.

"Forgive me, yes," Kosmo said. "I just wasn't expecting company."

He knew not to take a breath or endeavor to think. He

had been witness to too many poor saps who had lost their nerve and regretted it. So, in a single, fluid motion, he tipped back into the chilly air.

"Comrade Zablov," the voice from behind the door proffered. "This can all be very civilized."

THE HUNGARIAN'S KISS

"**Y**ou're certain?" Beryx Gulyas demanded, as he rubbed the turquoise and pyrite between his fingers. The minerals, according to his fortuneteller, aided digestion—and Beryx was suffering from terrible heartburn after eating smoked lard, washed down with a glass of *palinca* brandy for lunch.

"Yes, of course," Etor insisted.

Beryx hated to delegate his work. He'd spent too long and worked too hard to allow blunders to sully his reputation. He'd only delegated one other time and it had kept him up for two nights in a row, drinking a near overdose of morphine as he awaited word that the job had gone off fine. It wasn't without a hitch: the idiot Spaniard had left the woman alive, bludgeoning her with a silver-bound new edition of *The Conquistadors,* of all things, rather than using a pistol or a knife. An amateur should never get creative, Beryx Gulyas believed, and to him everyone was an amateur. Everyone but himself.

The woman was still in a sanitarium somewhere, cleverer than the leeches the doctors used on her bedsores, but not quite as sharp as the pigeons that perched on her windowsill. Gulyas would've done the job perfectly, but in fairness, the Spaniard's work had been adequate enough. The injured woman's husband never did openly challenge

Gulyas's boss, Nicolai Ceausescu, ever again, and the ambitious Romanian was elected to the Politburo less than a year later.

It was lucky for Beryx Gulyas—and it was luck, and not the Spaniard's skill—that the black hole of a vegetative state had an even more menacing effect on Ceausescu's nemesis than a clean kill. It dampened the man's ambition as surely as his wife's intellectual disfigurement snaffled his sexual attraction for her. It was, after all, their love of books that had brought them together, the man had explained to her doctor as Beryx lurked in the waiting room.

"You'd better be right," he told Etor.

Beryx slammed the phone down, chipping the cradle in the process. Etor was a lousy assassin, but the only assassin available in Greece—let alone Monemvasia—on such short notice. His effete tastes irked the Transylvanian native, especially since he knew Etor had spent most of his adolescence and early manhood as a rough for a Cretan gangster known as Baru. Now he sashayed around like he was better than everyone else and took assignments from Baru only when he was broke. Beryx would've made an example out of him if he were the big Greek, but there went Etor, eating his fancy food with his fancy girlfriends. Beryx Gulyas hated the Greeks almost as much as he hated the Romanians.

"Burn that little turd . . . " he said aloud before catching himself. He looked back into the living room and was relieved to see his Aunt Zuzanna was still asleep on the couch and hadn't heard his crass slip of the tongue.

Whenever Gulyas came to Brasov, he stayed with his Aunt Zuzanna, his uncle's second wife. She lived on the edge of the valley, where the gondola left hourly for the tops of the Southern Carpathian Mountains.

Zuzanna thought he was some big shot party official, and he proved her right by sending her twenty American dollars every month. It was a fortune for her and he was sure that she'd saved every dollar he'd sent and kept it buried in her yard somewhere. This simple pay-off allowed him the freedom to come and go as he pleased and discouraged his aunt from gossiping for fear of losing her meal ticket. These were the very practical reasons he sent her money. The personal reasons were more complicated.

His aunt had taught him how to make love some two and a half decades earlier. She was slender then and a youthful thirty. She had shapely calves, and full hips, and almost no bosom. At the time, she was perfection to him, and he would favor her physical type all of his life.

They had eight encounters total, but it was the first that was most exciting and played over and over again in his mind when he needed to summon the proper enthusiasm with his wife. He'd seen Zuzanna sunbathing in her yard, lying face down, with her bathing suit pulled slightly down over her hips so that just a wee bit of her cleavage showed at the top of her buttocks. He lost himself staring at her, and was startled when she called out his name and summoned him to her side. "There's some oil in the kitchen, would you bring it out here for me?"

He nodded yes and ran back into the house, retrieving the oil.

"Now, rub it on my back, will you?"

Gulyas bent over to cover his lap as he massaged the oil into her skin. Without any warning, she turned over and poured the oil over her tiny breasts and stomach. Zuzanna took young Beryx's hands and dipped them into the oil, guiding them over her body until he took over the motion himself.

"Such fine-looking eyes," she purred at him. "I could pluck one out and wear it on my finger like an emerald."

The tension in his loins became unbearable, and to Beryx's horror, suddenly released. Zuzanna giggled and he wanted to slap her. Instead, Beryx ran into the house and closed himself off in the cellar. It was quiet for several minutes there—he could hear no small, bare feet making their way into the house, and no voice giving gentle words of apology. Only the squeak of a fruit bat that had entered the house in a basket of freshly picked crab apples.

After little less than an hour, Beryx grew tired of the dark, damp cellar and made his way back to his room again. The house was quiet and still, and Zuzanna was nowhere in sight—neither inside in the kitchen, her usual place, nor outside on the lawn, where she'd been sunning.

It was to Beryx's great surprise when he opened his bedroom door and found Zuzanna, naked and asleep, on his bed. She pointed her toes and stretched a bit at the sound of the door, and slowly opened her eyes. He'd sworn she said 'come here' and he walked over to her shaking and fiddling with his trousers. Zuzanna helped him get undressed and then took over for the rest.

How different it was seeing her now. She'd become pear-shaped and had grown weary, having been shunned by her neighbors. Marrying a Hungarian was almost as bad as being one in those hapless years.

Zuzanna had tried to rekindle their affair once, but Beryx could no longer look on her with desire the way he had when he was seventeen and she was beautiful. He used his wife as an excuse, but Zuzanna knew the real reason behind his faithfulness. It was then that he started sending her money, and she started treating him like a nephew.

She dithered over whether he'd eaten enough and spent

entire days washing his laundry, trying to erase age-old stains from fine shirts that were too good to throw away. This was all done without affection, and Beryx now felt like a young boy with a distant mother when he was in her company. The hungry woman in his fantasies bore no resemblance to the busy, ashen woman who kept his underwear clean and smelling like freshly cut grass.

"Have you eaten?" she asked, without looking at him. She got up from the couch and pushed her feet into her slippers.

"I'm not hungry," he told her.

Regardless of their past, Zuzanna had never fully liked him, as she had never fully liked her late husband, Beryx's uncle by blood. They were, after all, ethnic Hungarians, and she was no Hungarian, as she'd liked to remind them—even during their most intimate moments.

"*Az apád faszát,*" he snarled to himself in Hungarian—*do it to your father's cock.* Beryx Gulyas fingered his ring—a bequest from his grandfather's time in the Royal Hungarian Army.

Though Beryx was born and raised in Transylvania, and carried a Romanian passport, he'd never felt like one of them, and the Romanians would never let him forget that he was by origin a Hungarian. Despite the overt snubs he'd endured throughout the years, his birth-country had not left him uninfected by its history and culture either. He loved the brittle air of the Southern Carpathian Mountains and the wide, sensual faces of the women who called them home. Their broad shoulders, made strong by carrying milk jugs, piles of pelts, and heavy buckets to and from the water pumps, were rippled from behind and particularly alluring when covered with perspiration. Romanian women sweat like their men and smelled like animals.

And there was a palpable sorrow present in even the

freshest newborn—a thirst for the agonies of life that courted lucklessness for the sheer thrill of surviving it. A Hungarian, though also drawn to the melancholy and macabre, might kill himself to end his grief, while a Romanian—particularly a Transylvanian—would hang on to the bitter end. Beryx Gulyas had a Hungarian heart, unable to truly love anyone except one of his own, but he possessed the soul of a Transylvanian.

"I'm going out," he said, as he retrieved the keys to his new Berlina from a wooden bowl by the door. He told her he wouldn't be coming back for at least a week, and would appreciate the holes in his trouser pockets being mended by then. It was a terrible inconvenience not being able to wear them, and they were his favorite pair—forgiving in their cut and capable of retaining their shape and crispness for hours longer than the other pants he owned. They also made him look at least five kilos slimmer.

Strangely, the pants meant more to him than the Berlina, which had been a recent gift from his boss. He'd "Oo'd" and "Aah'd" the way he was expected to, but a car was little more to him than a vehicle that got him from one place to another. Certainly, it spared him the inconvenience of having to take a bus or a train, but even at that moment, with his foot pressing the pedal to the floor and nothing but an empty, winding road ahead of him, Beryx did not feel the rush of adrenaline that consumed so many ardent drivers. There was only one thing that gave him that kind of rush.

A muffled groan pierced his reverie.

"Quiet!" he bellowed, and finally there was some peace in the car. Beryx had grown used to the incessant whining of the doomed over the years, but Leon Kunz, his regular pilot, had been begging since the Hungarian had returned to the car, repeating, "Please, no," over and over again in various intonations like an actor rehearsing his one big line. Although the moans were hushed by the trunk walls, they were beginning to wear on Beryx's already raw nerves, and he'd almost pulled over and shot the man like he had his co-pilot at the airfield.

"What have you done to yourself?" he'd demanded, as the co-pilot had begun slurring and sputtering that they weren't expecting him—no one had called. "You're too drunk to hear a phone, you mongoloid."

Beryx had broken their bottle of Boza on the concrete floor and carved the word *idiot* into the man's forehead before shooting him in the groin, stomach, and finally mouth. That was when Leon Kunz started whimpering and "Please, no," became the only words in his vocabulary. It was a common enough phenomenon amongst the very frightened—getting stuck, like a needle on a defective record album—but Beryx was in no mood for it tonight and was relieved that the German had been able to reign himself in. Now, he could sit at the wheel for a few moments after pulling over into the dead stillness of the mountain overlook, and think through what he wanted to do in the next twenty-four hours.

Anyone who had ever heard of Beryx in a professional capacity would know better than to lie about a botched job, but Greeks were unpredictable, and men like Etor had a far less exacting definition of success than a man in Beryx's position. He couldn't look Nicolai Ceausescu in the eye until he knew without a doubt that the American agent was dead and there were no loose ends to be tied up.

That realization changed his plans for the night. He tucked his gun into his holster, slipped on the thick, tobacco wool turtleneck Zuzanna had knitted for him, and stepped out of the warm car and into a freezing drizzle.

"Get up, Leon," Beryx ordered as he unlocked the trunk. Leon Kunz was rolled up into a ball with his face buried in his knees.

"Please, no," he started, and once he said it he couldn't stop.

"Leon,"

"Please, no,"

"Leon!"

"Please, no,"

"Shut up!"

"Please, no. Please, no. Please no."

"Leon," Beryx whispered, taking a long, deep breath. "I'm not going to kill you tonight, Leon. I'm not even going to beat you."

"Please, no."

"I'm an honest man, Leon. If you were going to die, I'd tell you. And if I was going to torture you, I would torture you. We wouldn't have to talk about it."

Leon Kunz stopped begging, but continued to cry, keeping his eyes closed tight and his kneecaps pressed against his brow.

"Let tonight be a lesson to you, Leon."

Leon Kunz nodded his head feverishly and vomited.

"Now take your stinking clothes off before coming into the car. It's almost dawn, and you're flying me to Greece in an hour."

Etor was not as stupid as Beryx had originally thought him to be. He was careless. He was trivial. But he wasn't an idiot, like Leon Kuntz's co-pilot had been, according to the crude carvings on his forehead.

"I shouldn't use so much salt," the Cretan gigolo reproved, helping himself to a liberal pinch for his baked eel. He had finished explaining to Beryx why he'd chosen to kill the American agent with poison instead of the sniper's rifle the Hungarian had championed, and was now looking forward to digging in to a costly lunch that wouldn't cost him a thing.

"What if you hadn't used enough of the toxin?" Beryx queried.

Etor shrugged and shook his head in the same manner he had used to dismiss their waiter when the young boy offered them another bottle of Retsina. The noonday sun was beaming into his eyes, but the gigolo wouldn't squint. It put his wrinkles on display.

"Then he would have died in three hours instead of three minutes. You only need enough to cover the head of a pin. And there's no antidote."

"Good," Beryx murmured.

Throughout the ages, poison had been referred to as "the coward's weapon," but the Hungarian assassin disagreed. Poison takes knowledge and a strong stomach. It can disfigure, distort and liquefy, forcing the perpetrator to watch an often gruesome process. It wasn't a coward's weapon, no, but it was certainly a feminine one.

"An Arab's Kiss, you called it."

"Arab's Kiss, yes. Very potent. Fast acting. It's cultivated from a type of passionflower that grows in the Middle East. They call it a . . . a . . . I can't remember, but it's a nice word. Beautiful. Like a woman's name—*Alehlah*."

Although Etor relayed all of this with his mouth full, he managed to avoid looking uncouth. He spoke equally with his hands, which moved in sensual, dancing motions and drew attention away from his lips.

"*Alehlah.* A very clever poison," Beryx acknowledged, and Etor smiled.

"Of course, if I'd used a gun, I would've been better prepared for circumstances created out of my control. If something or someone else emerged, I could've fired another bullet. The darts are more complicated. They're difficult to handle because you don't want the poison to come in contact with your skin." Etor stuck his fork into a heavily salted yellow potato the size of a walnut, and held it up while his tongue fished a piece of eel skin out of his back molar.

"But," he continued. "The fact is I've never liked blood. It's ugly and it stains the clothes."

Beryx knew how to get a man like Etor going. Initially reticent, the gigolo was growing more forthcoming with every glass of wine. All he needed to be assured of was a sympathetic ear, which would give him permission to bask in the sound of his own voice and boast an expertise in something other than luxury clothing and women's genitalia.

"Who could get in the way?" Beryx probed.

"I don't know. A lover, perhaps. Someone who wasn't supposed to be there."

Beryx moved closer to Etor, putting his hand on the gigolo's thigh. "A lover?"

Etor nodded and leaned in to the Hungarian, his lips brushing the curve of his ear. He didn't desire men sexually, in fact, he preferred the company of women on almost all occasions—but his days of picking and choosing were over, and men like Beryx Gulyas had deep pockets. "A very good lover," he whispered.

Beryx smiled, showing his teeth, which he didn't often do. Not out of vanity, although the state of his teeth was nothing to be proud of, but because it felt entirely unnatural to him. Smiling on command was difficult enough, but grinning was so contrary to his character that he looked more like an animal baring its teeth than a happy, amused human being.

"Then let's go to your place."

Etor pushed his plate away from him and leaned his elbows on the table. "My place is small. I'm not here very often. A couple of months here and there—mostly in the early summer."

"I don't like hotels," Beryx insisted. "They don't have kitchens. I must have a kitchen."

Etor shrugged, thinking, "Suit yourself." His Athens apartment was a depressing concrete matchbox of a place, and unlike Beryx Gulyas, he loved hotels. They were always so clean—the good ones anyway—and everyone did everything for him. "We should ask for a carafe of wine to take with us."

"Oh, yes," Beryx agreed. "In a glass carafe. Only a glass carafe will do. Because they're so *pretty*."

The Hungarian hadn't struck Etor as the type who cared much about pretty things, but then people often got very particular when it came to sex. And the Cretan didn't care if the man wanted a glass carafe or a glass giraffe, as long he got paid in American dollars. "I'll make sure to get the prettiest one."

Beryx smiled again and waved a hundred drachma note at the waiter. He got up to use the toilet, telling Etor he'd meet him outside. Having not had anything to drink, he didn't need to go, but he did need to purge himself of the heavy lunch he'd shared with the gigolo. Beryx was planning on having a nice dinner with a girl that night and wanted to save his appetite for his real date. He also wanted to look trim, and was depressed that he'd lost only two kilos. This, despite nearly starving himself on a diet of raw vegetables and vomiting every time temptation grew too great and he cheated with a sweet pastry or a sausage. He was sure to build up a good sweat with Etor, though. Maybe once he was finished with the Cretan, his pants would fit just a little bit better around the waist.

"Are you ready?" Etor cooed, pushing his shoulders back and sucking in his stomach.

Beryx Gulyas nodded. "Tell me," he said. "Do you have any salt at home, or will we need to stop at a market?"

"Ah, salt—it's good for the skin," Etor nodded, rubbing his palms over his chest.

"It's good for so many things," the Hungarian told him.

Adonia was clearly an invented name and Beryx imagined that the youngish woman the madam had offered him was born an Agatha or Acacia in some remote Greek fishing village. These thoughts about her were ruining his fantasy, and he swept them away as surely as he'd swept away the salt and broken glass on the floor of Etor's cramped city apartment. When he hired a woman for the night, he liked to pretend that they had met somewhere other than a brothel—in this case a bus stop—and would instruct the woman to bump into him and look up—or in this case down—into his eyes. She would feel an immediate and uncontrollable passion for him and agree to dinner, knowing full well that he intended to take her afterwards. She would love it and be anticipating it all night—frightened, ashamed, titillated.

"What's this place called again?" Adonia asked, gazing

up at the lighted Acropolis, which sat high above the tiny, outdoor restaurant her customer had chosen. Forgetting to act in his thrall, she recovered quickly by licking her lips and pushing her bust together, while she stroked his calf with her open-toed sandal.

"Socrates' Prison. The chicken is good."

"I like chicken," she cooed. "Do you like chicken?"

"Yes, I like chicken," Beryx breathed. From his pocket, he removed five stones with properties for bolstering will power—rose quartz, black onyx, rock crystal, chrysoprase, and tiger's eye—and lined them up on the table in front of him.

Adonia was just his type: Black hair, a small bust and soft, rounded hips. She would pucker her lips and whisper when she talked of sex—the way all of them did, the girls for hire. The way Etor had.

Etor. He'd been an idiot after all, Beryx concluded.

Not only had he admitted to leaving his gloves in his hotel room—discouraging him from loading another lethal dart if the need had presented itself—but he acknowledged leaving a witness behind.

"She's a harmless girl," he'd begged. "A tourist. I liked her."

He was adamant that she hadn't seen him and positive that she had nothing to do with the American agent professionally.

"They probably m-m-m-met somewh-where and ag-ag-agreed to m-meet for a p-p-private rendezvous," Etor had insisted. He was stuttering by then, so it took him a considerably long time to say what he needed to say.

"Then why wouldn't they meet in a hotel room?" Beryx had hissed. He'd left Etor's handsome face intact, but carved a Hungarian insult into him whenever the gigolo said anything stupid. *Geci* (asshole) joined *kurva* (whore), and *puhapōcs* (impotent), which were engraved on his buttocks, chest and thigh as Etor hung—arms above his head—from a water pipe in his kitchenette.

Beryx despised sloppiness in his line of work and took enormous pride in leaving no loose ends. He was particularly contemptuous of assassins like Etor, who took occasional jobs and wanted to get them over with as soon as possible— leaving behind bystanders because they liked them.

"Where," he had demanded, "is there room for favoritism in what we do?"

Etor hadn't been able to answer, as his throat was filled with nearly a pound of finely milled sea salt. The Hungarian had broken the Cretan's jaw, prying his fingers behind the man's teeth and pulling hard until he heard a crackling noise—like splintering wood—that made Etor shriek. It was a sickly sound that Beryx didn't like, but the gigolo was unable to close his mouth afterward, and it made pouring the salt down his throat a much easier task. Beryx was unclear as to whether the gigolo had died of cerebral edema— the most common outcome of salt poisoning—or asphyxiation, and wrote a note to himself to remember to contact the medical examiner and find out.

Whatever the case, Etor was gone and Beryx was glad. He was yet another black mark erased from Beryx's profession.

"I like the little lights around those poles," Adonia mused. "They're like twinkling stars." She never got to go to restaurants, let alone nice ones where a husband might take his wife.

"Those aren't poles," Beryx explained. "They're prison bars. For Socrates' Prison."

"Oh."

The waiter sauntered by, depositing two plates of chicken—broiled in an oily tomato sauce and accompanied by the small, yellow potatoes that Etor had liked so much. Adonia smiled and bit her lip, digging into the food with her knife and fork, and dripping grease from her lips into the hollow of what would have been her cleavage, if she had any breasts to speak of.

"So what did he do, the man who owns this place?" Adonia not only chewed with her mouth wide open, but spoke with it full. "You know, why'd he go to prison?"

"He didn't," Beryx enlightened her. "Socrates was a teacher who was poisoned in his prison cell a long, long time ago."

Adonia grimaced. "They name a restaurant after a guy who was poisoned? That doesn't seem very smart." It was only once Beryx heard her say a full sentence—without food in her mouth—that he realized she was no girl from a village. Adonia spoke a lower class Greek dialect direct from the Athens tenement slums.

"Ew, poison," she shuttered, looking down onto her oily chicken.

Beryx smirked and ran his crooked index finger from her elbow to her wrist, tracing it all the way down to the tip of her thumb. "Are you saying you have no craving for dessert?"

Adonia knocked back her glass of Retsina and slammed the empty pewter goblet onto the table with gusto. "Hell, yes I want dessert. I want baklava and strong coffee."

She laughed and tipped her ear to her shoulder, kicking off her sandal before wedging her foot between his legs and tickling his groin with her big toe. "Oh, and I want that kind of dessert, too. I've just got to go take a piss first."

Eying her ample bottom as she wiggled away from the table, Beryx believed in that moment that if he and Adonia had become acquainted under different circumstances—perhaps at a grocery store or in a doctor's waiting room—without her madam as a middleman, that she would've been with him tonight regardless of whether he was paying her. He could tell by the easy flow of their conversation, and by the way she looked to him for explanations about the simplest things. She wanted him, he was convinced, more than she'd ever wanted any man, and would do to him things she'd never done—even to her best customers.

"Excuse me, sir." The waiter bowed respectfully and presented Beryx with the key to an airport locker. "The young woman asked me to give this to you. She said not to worry, that a man with a mustache had taken care of her, and that you would know what she meant."

Beryx sighed, his fantasies shattered like the carafe of red wine he'd smashed against Etor's bedroom wall. It was time to go back to work, and Nicolai Ceausescu didn't pay him to have romantic encounters in foreign cities. He knew exactly what he would find in the airport locker: A photograph of his next mark, a schedule of his usual comings and goings, and a deadline. His Beretta was dirty now after the airport incident, so he'd have to procure another gun.

The Hungarian paid the check, leaving a little extra for the waiter, and hailed a cab to the airport. Perhaps on his next visit he could ask for Adonia again, and they could finally consummate their passion.

THE GREAT DETECTIVE

Rodki Semyonov was untroubled about letting the American girl get a few steps ahead of him. Russia, for all of its big cities and vast terrain was as small a place as any other police state. Especially for a first time visitor whose passport had been in the hands of a front desk clerk and now resided in Semyonov's coat pocket. She was an amateur, anyway. A rich girl who'd gotten in over her head and should've stayed on her vacation in Greece, instead of involving herself in situations she had no real imagination for.

General Pushkin would've preferred he had an encounter with the girl right away, but Semyonov opted for a more subtle approach. He hated to beat women. It was at times a part of his job, but he went to great lengths to avoid such confrontations. That was work for the secret police and KGB.

"The key sticks," the woman dressed as a maid told him, as she accompanied him to the tenth floor. She jiggled the lock before it released, letting him into the American woman's suite.

"She bought a green coat at a textile store near the Kremlin," the woman testified, "A bowl of sausage and pickle soup in the Red Square cafeteria, a coffee, two creams and no sugar, Kulich bread—though she didn't eat it—four vodkas, bear cutlets—of which she had only one bite—and stole a pencil from the front desk." One of ten assistants to the deputy head of hotel security, the woman was intent on distinguishing herself to the man she had always known by only one name—The Great Detective. "I was told she's a communist."

The Great Detective nodded. "So was she."

The woman didn't understand exactly what he meant, but pretended to, raising her eyebrow as if they were in on a very important clue together. But the Great Detective never returned the gesture and remained in the middle of the living room, his eyes fixed on a painting of a peasant woman in a pale, blue babushka. She reminded him of his mother.

"Comrade Detective," the woman entreated, "I hope it is not imprudent of me to tell you what an honor it is to meet you. If I can be of any help to you at all, I could go to my death a satisfied woman."

She hadn't intended on propositioning him, but his quiet demeanor and general ugliness had emboldened her. Had he appeared conceited, she would've never thought that a woman with her pleasant but ordinary features could interest him. Especially since men had often accused her of having a stern manner that lacked sensuality.

The Great Detective, for his part, gave no witty remark or double entendre. He simply buried his face in her hair and took her against a scratched up writing table. It's delicate, fawn-like legs clashed with the assistant's upturned thighs and ankles, and the Great Detective thought briefly that the writing table reminded him of his late wife. That thought alone made the encounter worthwhile.

When they finished, Semyonov helped the woman

restore her appearance, and with a sufficient amount of respect, asked her to leave while he performed his investigation. She saluted him before she departed—even clicking the heels of her walking shoes.

Semyonov liked being in a room so recently after its inhabitant had left. It allowed him to touch upon what his subject might have been thinking as well as doing. And most importantly, why? He caressed the nub of an open tube of lipstick with his index finger. Revlon, it read. He then wiped the waxy film on his trousers, leaving a crimson smudge. The American girl's toiletries remained largely untouched, and her bath, though wet, contained a couple of straight, black hairs. The floor in the bathroom had been wiped down, as had the path from the bathroom door to the sofa, and a white bottle containing a clear gel appeared to be the only grooming product she'd used. The detective didn't have to touch her bedding to see that it was wet.

At the bottom of her make-up case, underneath a disk of powdered rouge, he found a small mirror—the kind that could fit in a pocket book and be used to touch up lipstick. The Great Detective slid the mirror out of its embroidered linen sleeve and noticed that something remained inside the silk lining. Casually, he slipped his finger behind the lining and pulled out a metal card embossed with a plus sign, a star, and the Russian word for tree, *derevo*.

"Unless you have an urgent message for me, I would prefer to continue my investigation alone," Semyonov announced. The smell in the air had changed. It was infused with the scent of a man who bathed every day—an uncommon practice in Russia and most of Europe for that matter.

The Hungarian assassin put his gun away quietly.

"Pardon me, Comrade," the Hungarian said in Russian. "I met a girl at a party downstairs and she gave me her key. I hope something terrible hasn't happened."

"Are you from Bucharest?" Semyonov asked in Russian, and then repeated the phrase in Romanian, pocketing the metal card before turning to face the intruder.

"I'm Hungarian," he answered. "Here on holiday."

The Hungarian spoke in a distinctive Transylvanian accent. Semyonov had never been particularly good at speaking foreign languages, but he had an ear for detecting dialects. It was a skill he'd sharpened on the police force, when he'd been required to shadow visiting aliens.

"I've never been out of Moscow, but I encountered a student from Budapest once," Semyonov continued. "He sent me a recipe for stuffed cabbage that he wrote on cigarette paper and smuggled to me through one of the prison guards. He was crazy. I still haven't made the cabbage."

"Are you the house detective?" the Hungarian asked.

"Yes, I'm a detective." Semyonov yawned and cracked his neck, feeling an attack of bursitis coming on in his shoulder. "Most of my job is boring, but being sent after a nice-looking girl isn't so bad."

The Hungarian forced a smile.

"Can you tell me anything about her?" the detective inquired.

The Hungarian shrugged. "Not really. Pretty piece of ass. Throws her money around."

Semyonov continued to rifle through the girl's toiletries, picking through them one by one and lining them up on the bathroom counter. "Do you know where she gets her money?"

The Hungarian curled his lip and folded his arms across his chest. "Maybe her daddy," he replied.

Semyonov took out a small pad of poor-quality paper and made notes for himself in his own shorthand. There was an unmistakable clarity to finding the spigot of any investigation—the person from whom all of the answers would flow sooner or later, in one way or another. It was the same when he'd been investigating murders and black market rings, and was especially true now, when his detecting revolved solely around espionage.

"Must be her daddy," he agreed. "Say, you wouldn't want to have a drink with me, would you? Since your plans with the American girl have fallen through?" Semyonov's nose pointed left as he smiled, and the Hungarian was transfixed by the man's broken features. His interest turned to annoyance when the Russian detective put his arm around him and squeezed his shoulder.

The Hungarian shrugged him off and walked out of the suite. He knew it was imprudent to be rude—even to mid-level hotel employees—but he didn't plan on sticking around Moscow long enough to need any favors or fear petty repercussions.

The Great Detective, for his part, had expected the slight.

"Good morning," the pretty receptionist bid him as she checked her appointment book. The Hungarian nodded at her instead of returning the greeting. He hated speaking Russian.

As soon as he slipped the unmarked, bulging envelope into the mail slot, the girl found his name, saying, "Yes, here it is," and reached behind her for a towel, which the Hungarian rejected.

"I brought one," he explained and the girl told him to suit himself, but insisted he take her towel anyway. Rules were rules.

The Hungarian seized the graying rag and threw it to the floor as soon as he entered the bathhouse.

"Fabi," the Hungarian called to the preparatory masseuse. Fabi was dripping in perspiration—a pool of it having formed in a palm-sized ledge perched at the top of his domed belly. When he tipped forward to crack his knuckles, the pool dribbled over Fabi's middle and tinkled off the tip of his penis as if he were taking an unconscious piss. The masseuse then smacked his hands together three times, letting the echo bounce off the sopping tile walls of the steam chamber, and signaling to the Hungarian and a meaty woman who had come in behind him, that it was time for them to strip naked.

Fabi took the Hungarian first, slapping and pounding his back and legs, before grabbing his head in his hands and cracking his neck in two quick spins to the right and left. It was a sudden and unlikable way to be handled, but left the Hungarian feeling strangely titillated—much like he felt after completing a job.

With a slight bow, Fabi took the Hungarian's hand, shaking it hard, before moving on to the woman. She raised her arms over her head—as if she were being arrested—and the Hungarian watched the masseuse slap her breasts with a towel.

The key Fabi had given him was cupped tightly in his palm as he entered the next chamber. The Hungarian would've loved to bypass the rest of the gauntlet and head straight to the locker room for a rendezvous with his new gun, but once he entered the bath house, he knew there was no turning back or skipping any of its prescriptions.

With his usual resolve, the Hungarian looked out onto the four marble beds and chose the one closest to the single gas lantern that illuminated the chamber. He placed the key inside his cheek, laid down on his stomach and waited for one of the baton girls to come. To his chagrin, he got a fatty with yellow skin tone and sodden pubic hair.

"Take it easy around my bladder," the Hungarian ordered. He'd forgotten to use the toilet. The girl ignored him, and he watched her belly-folds waggle as she beat him with a club wrapped in a hot, wet towel until his muscles felt like noodles.

His luck in treatment providers got no better until he entered the fifth chamber, where he was oiled by a fair brunette. Fit and graceful, her only shortcoming was an engorged upper lip. She was also kind enough to use the loufa he provided instead of the ones dubiously sanitized by the house. He thanked her by patting her bare buttocks.

"Atta girl," he grumbled.

The Hungarian felt good and was especially glad that he'd chosen not to eat that morning. The gauntlet was a vigorous cleansing ritual that partnered well with a liquid diet and the Hungarian decided it was high time for a forty-eight hour reprieve from solid food. He entered the last chamber—the sauna—confident that his reflexes would be sharper and infinitely more precise due to his fast and looked forward to handing Fabi's son the key in exchange for a rolled bath mat that contained his new weapon.

"Hello there," a reclining man rasped, before clearing his throat and trying again. "Hello, I said. Fancy meeting you here." The ugly hotel detective sat up, leaning his elbows onto his knees.

"I'm sorry, have we met?" the Hungarian lied.

"Quite late last night. At the Hotel Rude."

The Hungarian leaned forward and squinted as if he was trying hard to place him. "Yes, yes of course. I'm not wearing my eyeglasses, so I didn't recognize you."

"Nor were you last night. You must be ashamed of them, like I am. I've yet to touch mine and they were imposed on me over a year ago." The detective sat up and leaned against the wall—his bent up face at odds with his body. Back at Hotel Rude, he'd looked rather lumpy in his overcoat, but here, naked and in unforgiving light, his physique revealed itself as lean and muscular.

"You lift weights?" he asked.

The Hungarian shook his head no.

"You should try it," the detective counseled. "It helps keep the weight off. Look at me—I'm over fifty, although I won't tell you by how much—and I don't look much different than I did twenty years ago."

He patted his taut abdomen and the Hungarian's face flushed.

"No, really," the detective continued. "I know it works. I fight—or at least I used to. What's more, I use a punching bag in the mornings."

The Hungarian sat down on the wooden bench facing the detective and stood up again. He looked out the small porthole of a window into the locker room, but Fabi's son was nowhere in sight. The masseuse had asked him explicitly to wait in the sauna until his son was ready for him.

"You should try it."

"What?"

"A punching bag," the detective clarified.

The Hungarian sat down again, crossing his arms over his chest. "I travel a lot," he mumbled.

"All the better," the detective prodded. "Pillows and blankets make decent punching bags, and it's much easier than finding weights—unless you don't mind lifting furniture. But I don't recommend that. You can strain your back."

The Hungarian nodded, looking out the porthole window again. "I'll take a crack at it," he grunted.

"Wonderful," the detective exclaimed. "Say, I could show you some moves. I've got time. Besides, lunch is coming up and what better way to work up an appetite?"

The Hungarian didn't answer his invitation.

"Don't you think?"

"Hmm?" Gulyas scowled.

"Punching works up an appetite, I said."

The detective put his fists up again and mimed a few fighting moves. The Hungarian stared numbly at his dodges and thrusts until Semyonov punched him with a right cross. It propelled him backwards onto the wooden bench, leaving him slumped nose to bellybutton. A few drips of water plunged from an IV onto the hot rocks, and a billow of steam obscured the Hungarian's head until evaporating into the parched air.

"Bombah!" Fabi's son, a frizzy-headed youth with a faint, black mustache and candy-red lips imitated the Great Detective's knock-out punch before pulling open the sauna doors. He took the Hungarian by the feet, dragging his sweaty body off the bench and letting his head thump to the floor and down the one step into the unisex locker room. The meaty woman from Fabi's chamber followed, still naked, but bone dry as if the heat had no effect on her. She carried a coil of steel wire and pulled up a chair—not for herself, but for the Hungarian, whom she proceeded to tie to it.

"Mr. Gulyas," the Great Detective urged, slapping the Hungarian's cheeks and dousing his face with a cup of coffee with cream that had been sitting on top of locker 32 since the early morning. "Are you ready for that drink now?"

Long before he became known as The Great Detective, Rodki Semyonov had harbored different ambitions. They were grand in neither scope nor mission, but they were ambitions nonetheless. He wanted his own apartment, where he could live with his wife, Polina, and not have to share space with a gaggle of relatives. He wanted a decent factory job in the burgeoning industrial town where he was born, and he wanted to have one child of either sex that he hoped would inherit Polina's earth-brown eyes.

The job had been provided for him, as he knew it would. A man of his size and strength was a welcome addition to most factory crews. Rodki was confident the child would come once he and Polina were settled. But obtaining an apartment for him and his family alone was another story altogether and Rodki Semyonov knew he would have to use his brain more than his back if he were to pull off such a coup.

"Az isten bassza meg a bu'do'sru' csko's kurva anya'dat!" the Hungarian, Beryx Gulyas, spat, spraying blood and a chipped tooth into Semyonov's face.

Semyonov broke the Hungarian's nose with the back of his hand for the insult. He didn't appreciate the visual of God "fucking his stinking, wrinkled whore mother," especially considering the way she'd died—in a gulag, he was told, buried alive next to his Polina.

It was his mother who had told him not to enter into the Shchelkovo underworld, but Semyonov had seen an opportunity for himself. The bare-knuckle tournaments that went on after the factories closed for the day promised big bucks, and more importantly, could win him some influence with the Housing Authority.

"It's illegal," his mother had warned. "Maybe they look the other way today, but tomorrow is always another story."

She was right, of course, but not about the fights. Those were protected by a man named Belnikov, who was at that time a favorite pet of Stalin's. Belnikov loved the tournaments and grew fond of the eleven-time tournament champion, whom he had personally nick-named *The Iron Knuckle.*

"Mr. Gulyas, I know who you are and what you do."

The Great Detective held the Hungarian's discarded Beretta above his bloody nose, letting him get a good look at it.

"It has an abnormal land and groove pattern, did you know that? It's a manufacturer's defect that makes it easy to track from a ballistic standpoint."

Beryx Gulyas eyed the gun, reacquainting himself with its blunt nose and quarter moon trigger. It had been cleaned.

"Antosha Sidorov, Lev Kretchnif, Teo Anghelescu, Anna and Magnus Karlsson, Charles Monks . . . I have thirteen other confirmations in addition to five other assassinations I suspect can be attributed to you, although no gun was used. It would appear you've branched out into other methods lately. Then, there was that unpleasant killing at the airfield which combined your methods. An improvisation, I suspect, since the co-pilot you savaged was the son of a German attaché."

Semyonov had always found interrogations distasteful, but they were a fact of life. There was nothing that made a man reveal his secrets or his character better than discomfort. Beryx Gulyas, of course, had no intention of disclosing any information no matter how badly he was beaten. Semyonov had encountered his type before, but their exchange wouldn't be for nothing.

"I'm confused, Mr. Gulyas, why you would be dispatched here to kill an American tourist when your prey is normally so distinguished?" Semyonov lit a cigarette and put it in the assassin's mouth. "You can't have fallen on hard times when there's so much work out there."

Gulyas spit the cigarette out and Fabi's son picked it up and began to smoke. It was a fine Turkish brand.

"Unless there's someone else you're after and the girl is incidental. I'd be careful about these incidental players, though, if I were you. You never know who they are."

Semyonov produced the metal card he'd found in the American girl's suite. He held it up close enough for Beryx to see and then put it back into his breast pocket. "Funny little thing—wouldn't you say? Your friend—the American girl—had it amongst her belongings. You wouldn't happen to know what it is, would you?"

Semyonov punched Beryx Gulyas in the kidney before he could answer. He bore down on the assassin's shoulder—not enough to break it, but enough to make the Hungarian wonder if it was broken.

"My biggest question to you, Mr. Gulyas, is—what now?"

It had become a stock phrase for Rodki Semyonov. He'd first used it on a British naval officer who was trying to pass himself off as a Kim Philby, ex-patriot, insisting that he was eager to betray his country and move to Moscow. Semyonov knew he was a spy the moment he saw him in his civilian clothes. Dressed to appear like a disillusioned member of the British upper classes, he wore a gold-tinted watch that he'd recently scrubbed free of tarnish and attached to a new leather band.

It was one of his first cases after being recruited into the Moscow police force. Belnikov felt they needed more good fighters on the force and thought "The Iron Knuckle" would be a boon at interrogations. He'd never suspected that Rodki Semyonov could be useful as anything other than a strong man, and Rodki Semyonov never suspected that his natural gift for puzzles and mysteries would draw him into Stalin's inner circle.

"Junior?"

The Great Detective stepped back and let Fabi's son box Beryx Gulyas' ears and kick his groin. The Hungarian bore the abuse well, so Semyonov took a couple of gentle cracks at him to make the eager youth feel like less of a light weight.

Long before joining the ranks of the Moscow police, where socialist protocol made mediocrity essential, Rodki Semyonov had learned not to flaunt his talents. It could be dangerous to distinguish oneself on the force, even if it was more results-focused than the postal service or the universities. Semyonov had always been a likeable fellow and figured out how to handle threatened superiors by using just enough working class humility and appearing genuinely surprised when he solved a case—as if it were by accident.

Belnikov wasn't fooled. "Aren't you a revelation?" he'd always remark when he visited Semyonov at his office. "Stalin has his eye on you."

It would appear Stalin had his eye on Belnikov, too: The trusted advisor's intestines were gored at his whore's apartment on New Year's Day in 1938—the same day they came for Polina and the rest of Semyonov's family.

Comrade Stalin felt he needed a personal detective

without any conflicting loyalties and in one stroke, Rodki Semyonov's personal life had ceased to exist.

"Mr. Gulyas, I'm sure you understand that whoever sent you—perhaps your Secretary General or one of his henchmen—is himself a servant of Moscow."

Semyonov clutched Beryx Gulyas by the hair and yanked his head backwards. The Hungarian, choked by his own blood, coughed and gurgled, taking deep gasps of air when the fluids from his nose drained to the back of his throat.

"All we want to know is why you're here," the Great Detective said. Like the Hungarian, he was bored. Both men knew a thing or two about applying and surviving pressure, so their encounter was becoming an endless game of tic-tac-toe.

Beryx Gulyas rolled his eyes into the back of his head as if he were about to have a seizure, but Semyonov would brook none of his dramatics. He beat the Hungarian with his knees and elbows until the man really was on the brink of unconsciousness, and perhaps, just the slightest bit sorry that he'd tempted fate with such a wise-ass move.

"You're looking tired, Mr. Gulyas," Semyonov teased. "I think you need rest."

Fabi's son was keen to continue the interrogation, but The Great Detective took him aside and explained how things were done. He wanted to give the Hungarian a bit of time to get his confidence back before he destroyed it again.

"I could use some lunch," Semyonov told Fabi. "Is there a decent cafeteria around here?"

Fabi told him there was, and directed him to a small greasy spoon nestled next to a book store. Semyonov bought a book of poetry by Mayakovsky and sat down at a window seat, ordering borscht and some boiled potatoes.

He opened the book and pretended to read. Thirty minutes—no more. That's what he would give the Hungarian, assuming, of course, that his soup was brought to him in a timely manner.

Fabi's son had a look of both surprise and determination frozen upon his face. His lips—no longer the color of cherry candy—had faded into a grayish-white, and blood ran in one smooth line from the pellet-sized hole above his right eyebrow into his hairline, where it disappeared. He was lying on the floor, clutching a baby blue towel with his left hand. His right hand—the one that had held Beryx Gulyas' Beretta—was empty, but his fingers looked like they were still coiled around the thing.

Fabi himself had been moved to one of the marble tables in the second chamber, where his big, round belly pointed to a vent in the ceiling. His brains remained in the first chamber, where they had already dripped down the wet, tile walls and slid towards the drain in the center of the floor. A blob of them jiggled over the drain, causing it to slurp.

"I'm leaving my key on the front desk," the receptionist informed. The noise of the drain made her queasy. She'd been in the toilet when Beryx Gulyas showed himself out, and had stayed there until The Great Detective returned from his lunch.

"I'm impressed with his accuracy," Rodki Semyonov told General Pushkin's aide, a nervous type who tried to cover his emotional frailty with an overdone military posture. Semyonov went on to explain that while Fabi's son had been shot at close range, Fabi had been a moving target who was blasted at a distance of several meters. That was no easy feat for a man who had been worked over as thoroughly as the Hungarian—a man whose eyes were nearly swollen shut, his body bruised to the bone, and his nose completely shattered. Semyonov held the aide's gun and followed what he imagined the Hungarian's movements would have been.

"Right there," Semyonov said, as he moved into the first chamber and found the angle at which Beryx had shot the gun-trading masseuse. Coming in from the second chamber, the Hungarian would've been totally exposed and Fabi would've had all of the advantages. There would have been no time to position for a shot—only a moment's grace to allow Beryx to aim by instinct and fire a single round.

"Perfect," The Great Detective whispered.

Beryx, he recognized, was the highest caliber of professional. Despite his skill, Semyonov could see why General Pushkin hadn't snagged him for his office, and let him continue working for one of the lesser states. Sadists had never bothered Pushkin, but instability did—and Beryx Gulyas's penchant for creative murder was a sign of both deep insecurity and staggering hubris.

If he could manage to stick to one method and do what he did best—as he had with poor Fabi and his son—he could have a long career ahead of him, Semyonov reflected.

"The General will be most unhappy about this development," the aide carped. "If they weren't already dead, he would have purged this operation of these two hacks and replaced them with more talented operatives."

Semyonov nodded. His special status left him largely immune from blame for problems like this. Fabi and his son may have been hacks, but they were KGB hacks and it was their responsibility to keep the Hungarian in line. If their superior had any common sense, he would've immediately noticed that this father-son team was a losing proposition. Semyonov had noticed. In fact, he had counted on it.

"What should I tell the general?" the aide implored. He tried not to seem worried about being the bearer of bad news.

"That I'll follow Mr. Gulyas and let the Comrade General know as soon as I discover anything."

The general held his cards close and hated to surrender any control. Semyonov knew, on the other hand, that surrendering a bit of control was precisely what broke a case wide open. The Hungarian would've rather died than talk, and all they would've gained by detaining him indefinitely was another prisoner. With Beryx Gulyas loose, Semyonov could wait for his movements as if he were monitoring a radar screen for a cloaked submarine. Eventually, it would have to surface.

"What if he disappears for good?" the aide moaned.

"It's possible, I guess. But trust me, my friend; I did quite a number on him. And he'll be far more likely to make stupid errors after the trauma of one of my interrogations—they take a lot out of man. You can tell that to the general."

The aide seemed pleased, jutting his chin forward and standing "at ease," while jotting Semyonov's exact words in his notebook.

"In the meantime, I'm afraid I may need permission to leave Moscow in the near future. It's just a hunch, but I'd rather the general give me authorization now instead of waiting until our friend reappears and risk losing him again."

It had been eighteen years since Semyonov had been allowed to leave the Moscow city limits. Stalin had guarded him so jealously that he hadn't even been allowed a visit

to the provinces and conducted all of his investigations—
no matter how far reaching—from the city proper. When
Stalin died and he acquired a new master, the restraints
upon his movements didn't change. But then, he'd never
questioned them, either.

Semyonov didn't know exactly what made him question
them today. He didn't want to leave Moscow. It had become a comfortable cell for him after all of these years. But
something inside him, something perhaps all too human
that had nothing to do with his desire or ability to solve
this case, made him want to get a look beyond his city
prison.

"One more thing," Semyonov added, as the aide looked
up from his notepad. "If I'm to follow this man myself, I'll
need a gun."

THE PERFECT MAN

The blood and broken glass on the vinyl floor of Etor's kitchen had been cleaned up, more or less—the largest pieces from the smashed carafe swept to the side and the sticky mess of body fluids swabbed with wet towels by a gang of grizzled and beefy Greeks. The men had performed their task in complete silence, not daring a glance at their master as he walked around Etor's mangled body.

"This is unspeakable," the Cretan gangster lamented, running his thick hand—made for chopping wood, spear fishing, and gripping a man at the throat—over his bald head. "What kind of animal would do this?"

Baru o Crete, as he was known, stood eye to eye with Etor, studying the death grimace on the gigolo's face as his gruesomely abused body still dangled from the water pipe in his kitchenette. The congealed blood had been wiped off Etor's smooth, tanned skin, but the gangster's men had yet to cut him down. He'd asked all of them but his man, Christo, to leave him alone with his boy. The men had filed out, one by one, as if in a funeral procession.

Until that day, Christo had been the only one who had known Etor was Baru's son. The two Cretans had grown up together, and Christo had been there when Baru became a father at thirteen. It was Christo's parents, and not Baru's mother—a notorious drunk and whore—who had raised Etor as if he were their own.

"He'll die a worse death, this Gulyas," Christo assured him, but both men knew Baru's fingers didn't extend very far beyond Greece. The Cretan didn't understand the Soviet Union and cursed himself for having taken a subcontract from one of their assassins. He thought he was doing his boy a favor by throwing him work and hoped the prospect of more plum assignments would lure Etor away from the folly of resorts and rich women and back into the folds of the family business. Baru o Crete could have finally introduced Etor as his son, instead of protecting him like he had and letting him have his fun. The Cretan gangster had thought he was being a good father, allowing his only son to indulge his fantasies, but what he'd feared had finally come to pass. Etor's frivolous pursuits were interpreted as weakness, and a more hardened predator had trapped and killed him.

"There's Zeki in Istanbul," Christo continued. "His men are appropriately vicious."

"But not very smart," Baru countered. There were at least a half dozen other gangsters with whom he was on friendly terms who either owed him a favor, or would've been happy to have a debt they could collect upon in the future. None of them were a match for a man like Beryx Gulyas, whose reputation had grown so fearsome in such a short period of time.

"He's not unbreakable," Christo said. "He just knows how to make a statement."

Baru took out his handkerchief and spit on it, using the cotton cloth to wipe the white dribble caked around Etor's mouth. On impulse, he tasted the sediment—salt.

"I know how to make a statement, too," the Cretan snarled.

Christo put his hand on Baru's shoulder and the gangster shuddered.

"You know what you have to do. He owes you a thousand debts and should be honored to get justice for Etor."

As any father would desire, as any Cretan would demand, Baru o Crete wanted the pleasure of at least watching Beryx Gulyas die, if not crushing his skull with his bare hands. But Baru's men were parochial Greeks, who spoke no other languages and had no heads for strategy. Hunting down a prized assassin required an international operation with ties deep within the Soviet Union.

"Get my boy down," Baru ordered, stepping away from his bloodied son. "I want to bury him myself."

"It was taken just this Christmas," Theron Tassos expounded, as he removed a photograph from his ostrich leather attaché case.

Baru o Crete adjusted the pocket square he'd hastily tucked into his jacket, its indigo dye leaving a faint stain on his fingertips. He dipped them in his tea and wiped them on a linen napkin before taking the Polaroid from his younger brother and holding it at a distance, to get a proper look. Baru hadn't seen his niece in nearly a decade and was struck by what a beauty she'd become. The sight of the color photograph—a rarity in his world—was equally impressive. He could even make out the eggplant tint of Lily's eyeshadow.

"She favors you," Baru commented, scrutinizing the picture further.

"You think so?" Theron Tassos dismissed him. The man Lily called Daddy looked hardly at all like his daughter. It seemed to him she had absorbed all of her mother's lovely features as she developed in the womb. Her high cheekbones and plump lips. Her wide-set eyes.

"She doesn't resemble you, but she does favor you," Baru insisted. "It's here," he said, pointing to the girl's nose. "And here," he continued, indicating her eyes. "It's not their shape, no, but what's behind them."

The two brothers nodded.

"Gulyas is his name, you say. That's Hungarian," Theron concluded as he slid Lily's picture back into its home in a plastic sleeve and restored it to his case. They'd been drinking tea for over an hour, having indulged in the kind of over-the-fence chatter that would've been impolite to forgo entirely. Even under these grave circumstances.

"No, he's Romanian. Perhaps a Hungarian by family origin."

Theron knelt down on two of several Turkish pillows that were strewn about Baru's living room, and the Cretan gangster followed him. "And it's important to you that he suffers."

"More than Christ," Baru hissed.

Theron put his hand on Baru's bald head. His hands weren't as lethal as his brother's—made for holding weapons, not being them—but possessed the even touch of a man long accustomed to power. "No one can suffer more than Christ."

It would've been sacrilegious for him to contend otherwise, but Theron Tassos had indeed made men suffer much more than Christ. Christ, it could be argued, had the added burden of humanity, which made his suffering infinitely greater from a spiritual perspective, but pain is pain when you're made of flesh and blood, he believed.

Etor himself had once narrowly escaped one of Theron

Tassos's punishments after he'd been late with a one-time delivery to an Oriental. It was a small order from a bit player in an even smaller country, so it was just as easy for Tassos to tell Etor to get lost and stay lost than it was to teach him a lesson.

But he'd never forgiven Baru for his poor judgment. The two, who had once been as close as soldiers in a death battle, had become distant in the seven-odd years since the Etor incident. While they'd never officially fallen out with one another, they hadn't spoken in all of this time, either.

"Do you wish to be present?"

Baru exhaled and closed his eyes for a moment. "Oh, yes," he whispered.

Whatever their conflicts over family and business, a Greek would never deny a brother his revenge. Especially over the death of a child—no matter how disappointing that child might have been.

"Do I know the man you'll use?" Baru asked. The Cretan's eyes were leaden and glassy, bearing the look of an old man's eyes in the long year before his death.

"I'd never use a Greek," Theron insisted. "He must be a Russian. I never trust anyone but a Russian to inflict pain."

Baru straightened his shoulders and swallowed hard, as if confronting his first glimpse of Etor's mutilated body. "This Gulyas. He's no Russian, yet he's built a savage name for himself."

Theron Tassos lit a cigarette and shrugged. He knew that men like Beryx Gulyas came and went all the time—burning bright for a few short years before descending back to earth—or rather, beneath it. Sadists rarely lasted very long. Egoists let their vanity override their intellect. Gulyas had both marks against him.

In the arms dealer's experience, it took an impersonal character—someone imminently flexible, who took neither pleasure nor pain from his work—to last for any meaningful length of time.

"Don't worry," he said. "I have the perfect man in mind."

Victoria Dougherty

Victoria Dougherty is the author of The Bone Church. She writes fiction, drama and essays that revolve around lovers, killers, curses and destinies.

Her work has been published or profiled in the New York Times, USA Today, The International Herald Tribune and elsewhere.

Her blog – COLD – features her short essays on faith, family, love and writing. WordPress, the blogging platform that hosts some 72 million blogs worldwide has singled out COLD as one of the top 50 Recommended Blogs on writers and writing.

Currently, Ms. Dougherty lives with her family in Charlottesville, VA and has recently completed The Hungarian, her second in a series of Cold War themed historical thrillers.

Follow COLD at www.victoriadougherty.wordpress.com

It's bling for your soul!

Daring escapes, backyard firing squads, bowlfuls of goulash, gargoyles, gray skies and bone-chilling cold. From the author of *The Bone Church* and *Welcome to the Hotel Yalta* come these confessions of a Cold War princess.

Get your FREE copy here:
http://victoriadoughertybooks.com/get-your-free-book/

Printed in Great Britain
by Amazon